DRAWING BLOOD

BOOK ONE
THE RELICT SERIES

LONO PUBLISHING
Encino / California

DRAWING BLOOD
BOOK ONE
THE RELICT SERIES
relictbookseries.com

Copyright © 2012 Richard Finney
Published by Lono Publishing
Lonopublishing.com

Book Cover Photograph © Vittorio – Crescenzo Salatiello

ISBN 978-1-938457-02-9
Second Edition
Printed in the United States of America

Praise for Author Richard Finney

———

"***Demon Days*** delivers suspense and pacing that rivals a James Rollins thriller, with stabs of visceral horror worthy of Douglas Clegg and Brian Keene."
—John Kirk, author of *The Talion Moth*

"***Demon Days*** by Richard Finney is a fresh and rich approach to the age-old battle between good and evil. It's a gripping, visual, pulse-racing read."
—Andrew Neiderman, Author of *The Devil's Advocate*

"Like the best of T.E.D. Klein, ***Demon Days*** builds to an awe-inspiring confrontation between our thoroughly modern sensibilities and the supernatural. Finney will have your full attention right up to the last word."
—Joe McKinney, author of *Apocalypse of the Dead*

"I started recommending ***DEMON DAYS –Angel of Light*** not long after I started reading it and it will be a hard novel to forget."
—Shannon Pease, *Good Reads* Book Blogger

"***DEMON DAYS –Angel of Light*** is fast-moving and enthralling. You will find yourself completely entranced as you are reading it. The characters in this novel are beautifully developed and distinct. There is an extremely intricate plot with twists and turns and sudden betrayals – you just couldn't ask for a better book."
—Katy Sozaeva, *Now is Gone* Book Blogger website

Richard Finney

To Brooke, who knows this storyteller's favorite words - "And what happens next…"

Franklin Guerrero

To Debbie, my world, and my most important audience. I couldn't do it without her.

"Relict" rel·ict (noun) – *1. A species or organism surviving long after the extinction of related species or organisms. 2. A once widespread natural population surviving only in isolated localities because of changes in the environment. 3. A remnant of a preexisting species left behind after a destructive event has taken place.*

CHAPTER ONE

For most of his life, all Matt Haynes thought about was himself.

After the takeover, he took some time to think about the fate of the rest of the world.

But those thoughts didn't last very long.

He did think about his ex-wife, Beth. And at least those thoughts lasted long enough for him to work through a plan to make it back to the States.

That was why he was riding a motorcycle on one of the back roads leading to Morristown, New Jersey.

He and his buddy, Jay Granville, had made it a point to steer clear of any of the main highways. Matt was convinced this had helped them avoid any confrontation with any of the patrols as they travelled through four states.

Jay let go of his right handle grip, then balled the same hand into a fist and extended it high in the air. Matt triggered the brakes on his motorcycle, rolling to a stop next to Jay's bike.

Seven cars were left abandoned in the middle of the road ahead. There was also a minivan, which had somehow wound up stuck in a ditch, its rear tires hanging at least three feet off the ground.

"What do you think?" asked Jay. "Ride on… or check and see if there's anything we could use?"

"We're not very far away from Beth's house," Matt said.

Stopping less than a mile away from his ex-wife's house would only mean opening up the possibility of one of the patrols seeing them. He knew if that happened, he'd go to his grave thinking about the irony of coming halfway across the world only to be stopped a half-mile away from his goal.

But he voiced none of this to Jay. His buddy had been with him since Madrid and he didn't want to feel like he was the one calling the shots.

"Where did these people think they were escaping to?" Jay turned to him. "You know what I'm talking about?"

Matt nodded. "Yeah, I hear you."

"Like there was someplace better to run off to…"

He turned to look toward the horizon. The sun was setting. Matt took off his shades. He actually squinted as his eyes adjusted to the dying light.

"I'm low on munchies," said Jay. "How much you want to bet that even though the world was coming to an end, no one wanted to die starving to death? There's got to be something to eat. And we know the bloodsuckers wouldn't have a reason to take it."

"Yeah, okay, that makes sense," said Matt. The last thing he wanted to do was argue with Jay after he had come all this way with him. "Let's go take a look."

They switched off their engines and walked their two bikes over to the side of the road.

From his leather bag, Jay grabbed a sawed-off shotgun, the one he had pulled off the dead guy who was working with the toll gang who had tried stopping them near Raleigh.

This time Jay didn't bother taking the rifle out of the blanket. Between his finger and the trigger was a baby-blue, dyed-cotton quilt that a woman in the Sudan had given Jay for saving her husband from a government death squad.

Matt had a 9mm Beretta Px4 in a shoulder holster strapped across his chest.

He had originally picked up the Beretta in Libya, during the overthrow of Gaddafi. Ten days ago he paid off the customs guy in Atlanta to let him leave the airport with it.

The crocodile-leather shoulder holster (with cognac ostrich trim) was something he had snatched forty-eight hours ago while he and Jay were squatting in a condo in Norfolk, Virginia. The holster was hanging on a wall hook, only a few feet from a body. Matt surmised that the dead man had tried to crawl across the carpet in a futile attempt to reach his weapon.

Jay marched across the blacktop toting his shotgun with the confidence one usually reserves only at sunrise as Matt, one by one, checked the cars left abandoned in the middle of the road.

His buddy had it right – escape to where? The whole world had come under siege. As Matt was in the middle of going through the trunk of the seventh vehicle, he tried to fathom what any of the occupants in the cars must have been thinking on the day they loaded up all their belongings and headed from their home.

"Anything?" Jay whispered to him from a dozen feet away.

"Nothing. Someone's already been through here."

His words didn't upset Jay; they brought a smile to his friend's face. The discovery had confirmed, at least to Jay, what he had been hoping for ever since they landed in the States on one of the last military planes.

"The States are the only place where I can imagine anyone will put up a fight."

Matt disagreed with Jay's narrow assessment of who would and would not put up a resistance to the takeover. But he wasn't about to argue with the only man willing to watch his back as he made his way to New Jersey to check on Beth.

"Must be the resistance, " said Jay, walking parallel to Matt as they headed toward the last car, the one abandoned on the side of the road. "They're the only ones who would give a shit about real food."

It was impossible for Matt to ignore the sight of Jay walking with an extra bounce in his step. He was clearly excited to pin some hope on the idea that there was a group of resistance fighters giving it back to the vampires.

Matt approached the last car, the minivan stuck in the ditch. The back trunk door was open and raised, and though he had to stand on the balls of his feet to look inside, Matt saw the belongings in the back had already been rifled through.

Jay suddenly raised his fist, prompting Matt to freeze.

The two stood still, both listening to their surroundings, waiting for any sign of an impending attack…

When more than a minute had passed, Jay lowered his fist and Matt made his way toward the front of the car.

What he saw surprised him. Unlike the other vehicles they had searched, this car still had two bodies: adults in the driver and passenger seats.

The brain matter splattered on the window behind the passenger made it easy for Matt to deduce that she had died from a head shot fired at close range.

The gun that had done the damage was in the lap of the male driver, inches away from the hand that had pulled the trigger a second time. His brains were above his head on the interior ceiling of the car.

Then Matt noticed something.

He quickly stepped away from the vehicle, waved his hand in the air for Jay to see, and pulled out the Beretta from the shoulder holster.

Jay followed alongside as Matt moved with a purpose back to their motorcycles. "What did you see?" whispered Jay.

".38 Special. Two gunshots. Two victims. Both dead... *dead*... that's why they were left behind."

They were moving double time and Jay's breathing was louder than his question. "And what else did you see?"

"No blood," Matt whispered. "Not a single drop..."

CHAPTER TWO

"See anything?"

Matt didn't immediately respond to Jay's question as he stared through a pair of night-vision binoculars at his ex-wife's house.

Finally, he turned and walked back toward their parked motorcycles. Along the way, he handed the binoculars to Jay.

Beth's house was across the road: about three hundred yards across from where they had parked their bikes, in a part of the woods that was so dense not even a high-beam light from a helicopter would have been able to spot them.

"Okay, I see why you're not so chatty. But just because there aren't any lights doesn't mean your ex-wife isn't alive."

"Look at the motion-detection lights near the garage," said Matt. "If they were operative, we would see a small, flashing, red light."

He panned the binoculars across the one-story, mid-century, ranch-style house. It was pitch black, not only around the entrance to the garage, but the whole front of the house.

"And you know about the motion-detection lights how?"

"I installed them myself."

The last time Matt had seen Beth was more than nine months ago. It was possible she could have had someone change the lights. But why? An ex-wife changes the locks on the doors to their house, not the motion-detection lights in front of the garage.

"Maybe the guy who replaced you didn't like how the lights kept him up at night when every cat, raccoon, or rabbit strolled by."

When he didn't get a response, Jay lowered the binoculars and turned to look over at Matt.

Matt was rubbing black shoe polish all over his face.

"Looks like you already made a decision," said Jay as he walked back toward the motorcycles. "Mind letting me in on the plan?"

Matt tossed the tin of shoe polish back into the leather satchel on his motorcycle and reached in to grab something else. It was something he snagged from a sailboat anchored just beyond a harbor in Rhode Island.

"A flare gun? This is bullshit."

He was hoping for a clean exit, but the outrage in Jay's voice caused Matt to slowly turn around.

Jay was holding up the flare gun as if it was the perfect piece of evidence of his outrage.

"I'm sorry I got you involved in this."

Matt's words caused Jay to lower the gun.

They had been together for the last ten years in at least half a dozen hot spots across the world and Jay had never once heard Matt utter the words -- "I'm sorry."

"I would ask for one last favor. If you see any of the bloodsuckers moving toward Beth's house, you fire the flare gun. Then get the hell out of here. Just west of here there's a canal system that goes on forever. You might be able to lose any patrol coming after you."

"I have a better plan. Why don't we both tub-thump your ex's house and we'll deal with any patrol along the way."

Matt shook his head.

"My ex-wife… My suicide trap. I don't want you joining the parade of people I see when I'm asleep. Okay?"

He didn't wait for Jay's reply. Matt turned and started walking away.

"So… I guess the threesome with your ex-wife I've been fantasizing about all this time is definitely off?"

Matt cracked a smile at Jay's remark, but he never broke his stride as he disappeared into the darkness of the surrounding woods.

After running more than a mile through the woods, the edge of the forest facing his ex-wife's backyard snuck up on him. Matt barely caught himself before he walked right into an open area.

He took a moment to look around to see if he was being watched. His effort was perfunctory. If one of the vampires were keeping an eye on the house, it would have had no problem seeing him in the darkness.

Then Matt scrambled across the open field to the wire fence – barely five feet high – which encircled Beth's property.

A few weeks after they had moved into the house, Beth had a landscaper put the fence up to keep deer from getting into the backyard and eating all of the bushes she eventually would plant herself.

Matt hopped over the fence and sprinted across the lawn. When he arrived at the back door to the house, he stopped to catch his breath.

At his feet shards of glass sparkled in the moonlight. Matt saw that the window in the door had been shattered.

He rose slowly, just high enough to look above the open wooden frame. Nothing. But if this was a trap, he hardly expected it to be sprung in Beth's garden room.

He pushed open the door while at the same time holstering his Beretta. Even with just the moonlight shining through the garden-room glass, he could see that all the potted plants and trees were dead. Dead for several weeks.

Through two tours in the Middle East, and a stint working as a paid mercenary soldier by a security company, his wife had been able to maintain the beauty of the garden room.

When he entered the living room of the house, he switched off his flashlight.

The curtains normally covering the front window had been ripped down, allowing plenty of moonlight to spill in.

The room had been overturned, like a team of burglars had their way with the contents.

For the first time since he had landed in the States, Matt finally started to believe something that he had dared not think about.

His entire trip had been a fool's errand.

An object on the fireplace mantle caught his eye and Matt walked toward it.

It was an antique jewelry case with a painted, lead-glass top and sides. Matt opened the lid and discovered gummy bears inside. He couldn't help but smile.

When he and Beth were still together, they would do grocery trips together. His wife would inevitably buy a ton of gummy bears. And each time, after unloading the groceries, the gummy bears would mysteriously disappear.

One day he discovered the stash – in the glove compartment of their car.

"Of course they're in the glove compartment of the car. That's where I like to 'bake' them while the car sits in the sun."

Once they were properly "baked," Beth would put them in the jewelry box.

Matt squeezed one of the gummy bears. Rock hard.

Beth was dead.

Convinced for the first time Beth was really gone, all Matt could hope for was that she was dead… DEAD.

Suddenly, there was a noise. Matt dropped the gummy bear as he crouched down and withdrew his Beretta.

CHAPTER THREE

Matt moved as silently as he could toward the noise. He wasn't sure, but he thought it came from behind a living-room door that led to the basement.

As he stepped quietly, Matt passed across a large mirror hanging on the wall. He caught a glimpse of his unshaven face underneath the dark shoe polish and saw that his normally close-cropped hair had grown out at least two inches since he had left Asia to fly back to the States. Now it looked unruly and matted with sweat and dirt from the motorcycle ride through the east coast.

But it was the taut skin against his cheekbones and the hollow look in his eyes that made Matt stop in his tracks for a second, as if he had stumbled across the intruder who had made the noise.

He pressed his ear against the basement door, but didn't hear anything. Taking a few moments to collect his nerves, Matt then threw open the door.

A beam from a flashlight hit his eyes, causing him to quickly decide -- either fire toward the source of light or move for cover.

He ducked out of the doorway.

Then he called out, "Beth?"

"Who's there?"

It was a male voice, slightly above a whisper. But before he could respond...

There was the sound of a muffled gunshot.

Looking in the direction of the noise, Matt saw through the living-room window a bright-red flare emerge from the woods, then arc across the nighttime sky.

It took every ounce of self-control Matt had accumulated in the last few years to calmly put his gun back into its holster. He raised his hands and calmly stepped back into the doorway.

Whoever it was in the basement lowered his flashlight after a few seconds.

It allowed Matt to finally see who was standing at the bottom of the short stairway. He could also see all around the intruder were open boxes that had been rifled through.

"What are you doing down there?" asked Matt.

"Keep it down or you'll attract a patrol."

"They're already here. This is your last chance. Where is Beth?

"I'll take you to her. Just shut the fuck up!"

Thump!

The noise came directly above Matt. Someone - or some*thing* - had landed on the roof.

The man in the basement clicked off the flashlight.

Matt quietly closed the basement door. There wasn't a sound of protest from down below.

He retreated into the shadows until his back was flush against the living-room wall. Matt stared up at the ceiling, imagining the silent steps the vampire was taking across the roof toward the skylight.

Then he kept his attention fixed on the glass.

Suddenly, the skylight shattered.

Matt didn't look away or flinch. He fired five shots. The first two hit the target, but the third managed to change the trajectory of the vampire's descent. The final two slugs made sure its landing was at the far end of the living room.

He did not take any solace in the silence. Matt's eyes stayed fixed, and his gun was still aimed at the completely still creature lying on the living-room carpet, highlighted by a shaft of moonlight coming through the living-room window.

The stillness was broken by the sound of a motorcycle engine. The sound was drawing closer, not growing more distant.

Suddenly, the vampire flashed open its eyes – the pupils were enlarged and black like they were transplants from a shark. Then the creature opened its mouth, exposing elongated incisors glistening in the moonlight.

Matt didn't hesitate. He sprinted across the living room and leaped over the vampire just as the creature made a move to stop him.

Beth's living room window exploded outward.

Matt landed on the front lawn, with thousands of pieces of glass trailing right behind him. His landing was awkward, but on two feet. He touched down, leaning forward, enabling him to roll into a somersault, which he completed only in a way that demanded that he roll into another.

Instead he stumbled forward… and began to run. He looked behind him once, but that was only cursory. Matt was moving as fast as he could toward the sound of the motorcycle engine.

He leaped over the hedge that ran across the front of Beth's house. His perfect landing was highlighted by the beam from a motorcycle's headlight.

Jay skidded his bike to a stop.

"I can't believe you saw the flare…"

As he hopped on behind him, Matt saw Jay was wearing a pair of night goggles

"I told you to head west…"

"Yeah, well, west runs right past the house."

Jay let his foot off the clutch and the motorcycle took off.

Their motorcycle was weaving through the narrow, twisty, tree-lined road through the Morristown suburbs. It was where Matt grew up. And it was where he hoped he could eventually raise a family.

But now all he could think about was how it was just another place for the vampires to occupy.

"How many did you see?" Jay shouted into the wind.

Matt responded as he ejected the spent clip from his Beretta.

"Just one."

"Then maybe it wasn't a vampire. Maybe it was just your ex-wife's divorce lawyer. Didn't you say he was always out for blood…?"

Matt slammed another clip into his gun, expecting to hear Jay's self-satisfied chuckle at his own joke, but it never came.

Instead, Jay's body stiffened… and then the motorcycle began to slow.

Ahead of them was a blockade made up of several large military trucks, and a dozen figures standing in front of the vehicles.

From their distance it was only Jay, wearing the night goggles, who could confirm what Matt suspected was before them.

In the night scope the heat pattern of a bloodsucker registered as blue.

"Vampires…"

Jay released the brakes and steered the motorcycle into the surrounding woods.

Their motorcycle was doing a "shake and rake" through the trees – bouncing on a bumpy, dirt path, with branches whipping across their heads and bodies.

"Buddy, we can't outrun them. So don't try…"

His caveat had the opposite effect on Jay.

"Wanna bet?"

He twisted the right handgrip and the bike picked up speed.

Matt turned to look for any signs they were being followed.

On his right, he saw a shadowy figure moving on a parallel course with their motorcycle. The only reason he saw the creature was the wake of bushes and trees the vampire left behind as it streaked through the woods in pursuit.

He fired a couple of shots from his gun. Matt was surprised to see that he must have hit something, because the parallel movement through the woods suddenly stopped.

Matt turned his attention to the other side and immediately spotted two streaking shadows cutting two paths through the woods.

He switched his Beretta to his left hand and fired several shots, then ejected the spent clip from his gun. But before he loaded another clip, Matt noticed that the two vampires that had been trailing him… had stopped.

It was too easy. Something was wrong.

He tapped Jay's shoulder and shouted, "We're being guided into a trap."

A dark shadow suddenly appeared in Matt's periphery vision.

"A trap! What are...?"

Before Jay could finish his sentence, the shadowy figure swept across Matt's line of sight.

And Jay was gone.

His buddy was no longer sitting in front of him, guiding the motorcycle. Matt's lightning-fast reflexes had saved him in the past, but as he lunged forward to grab the handle grips of the bike, the front tire of the motorcycle hit a dirt mound and the impact sent the unmanned bike skyward.

Somehow, in midair, everything slowed down. He was able to see a dark shadow move toward him a split second before the figure collided with him.

Then everything seemed to speed up again.

Matt hit the ground. Pain shot through his entire body. And it took him a few seconds to see again in the dark.

The figure that had grabbed him in midair was underneath him. Matt tried to see the face... but everything around him was blurry...

He reached out his hand and suddenly realized he was alone, lying on his back in the dirt.

There were voices just a few feet away, but no matter how hard he tried, he could not turn his head to look in the direction of the voices.

"This one is dead because of your stupidity!"

"I protected him with my body just as we planned."

"This wasn't anything like we planned!"

There was silence and Matt wasn't sure if what he heard was real or not.

The ground near him shook.

Someone dropped to their knees right next to him.

"You stupid fuck! Wipe the blood off your lips. The last thing we want is anyone back at the camp to see how you indulged yourself in your mistake."

He thought he recognized the voice.

Again Matt tried to turn his head to see who was speaking, but just as he was finally able to look toward the voice, everything grew dark.

Then everything went to black.

CHAPTER FOUR

MORRISTOWN COURIER

Local Man Missing

By Brooke Skulski

Morristown police are concerned that Ian Haynes, 24 years old, has not been seen for the last two weeks and they are now turning to the community for help.

"There is a real concern that something has happened to this young man," said Morristown police Lieutenant Ralph Steedman. "We're hoping that perhaps someone out there knows something that will help us locate him."

Haynes was last seen by his parents when he left their house to drive to Essex Fells to compete in a chess tournament. His parents, Bud and Elaine Haynes, have told police that their son was not the type of person who would just suddenly disappear without an explanation. "My son put off going to college when both my wife and I had health problems in the last few years," said Bud Haynes. "He would let us know if he was just driving to the corner store to get some milk."

On April 21st, Ian Haynes left his parents' house after dinner to compete in the county finals of the "Check Mate Chess Competition," sponsored by the internationally known chess organization, CMCC Worldwide. He traveled alone to Essex Fells, a short fifteen miles away, and his parents believe he was not planning on meeting anyone along the way.

Haynes's car, a red Honda Civic, was found just three blocks away from the Radoff Hotel, where the tournament was being held. CMCC officials told police that Haynes never checked in for the competition.

"We were mystified when his match came and went without any word from him," said CMCC official Winston Gaiman. "I know Ian personally and knew how much this tournament meant to him. When he did not show up, all of us feared the worse."

Ian Haynes attended Morristown Royal high school, where he won several academic awards as well as receiving academic scholarships to three different Ivy League schools upon graduation.

"He graduated valedictorian in high school, participated the last few years in several local charities, and was just a few days away from beginning his first semester at Columbia University. We believe this is not a young man who would just run away to begin a new life," said Lt. Steedman.

The missing man's parents have posted a $5,000 reward for any information leading to their son's whereabouts. Anyone who might have information should contact the Morristown police department and ask to speak with Lt. Steedman

IAN HAYNES' JOURNAL

I wish everything I wrote was more than just statistics.

But that's what you become really great at after you've been turned.

Statistics.

No notes. No calculators.

You have a perfect recall of facts, figures, or events in a timeline.

In fact, a timeline is our specialty.

When all you do is... exist.

Remembering the dates, names, achievements, failures of the living is not a problem.

I'm like a computer that never needs to be rebooted.

Perhaps the best way for you to understand what I have become is to stay just with the stats.

There are over 221 "Blood" camps in "North America."

210 in "Europe."

Those working in "Asia" have got to be concerned. Only 43 camps so far.

The latest official line from the committee is that at least seven of those camps aren't even extracting blood from donors because everyone they test flunks the most basic redlines.

And that's the "Official Line!"

Yeah, right now I'd be thinking "eternity" is not so locked in if I was stationed in one of the blood camps in Asia.

According to Winston the "unofficial line" is everyone is scared shitless.

Of course no mea culpa, official or unofficial, from anyone on the committee about how they obviously miscalculated about setting up blood camps so close to where all the bombs went off.

We all saw the explosions: some of us on TV, others firsthand. What was the VC thinking? That there would still be people we could tap?

Here's an idea; we should have made everyone on the committee who wasted resources building those camps be the first to get off on the radioactive juice.

I know Winston feels the same way.

He often talks derisively about the Second Seating. He refers to them as "VireArchII," but to me, they're all just part of the same "Vampire Committee."

"Watch what happens," Winston said to me. It was just a couple weeks before we moved from the shadows to take over control of the world. "Politicians of the living will say anything to save their career; a vampire will promise anything to save his, and he has all of eternity to make good on his promise."

But even Winston was shocked as we pored over the official worldwide estimates of the living. Clearly the VC had drastically underestimated how many would be left standing after the takeover, and I could detect a glint of paranoia in his eyes. This was a rare sight. Over all the years I've known him, Winston seldom allows his existence to be influenced by fear. His favorite quote from Laski Weldon — "The living are consumed with the prospect of dying, and therefore fear informs their existence. Our kind has no such concerns, and that is what we must dwell on so we can always feel alive."

I have had the benefit of his wisdom for a relatively short period of time. And his depth of knowledge has been vital to my new life. His words are often chosen from those of our kind who he has shared the shadows with for nearly a thousand years. "Wise are the ones who have seen what lies on the road ahead. But the wisest are those who can also look into your eyes and understand where you've been."

My master is one of the wisest of our kind. What Winston has taught me continues to inform all my actions, even if at times I don't always understand what lies behind the long history that underlines each of the words.

I was not surprised when the committee requested that he serve as commander of the Coagulation Concentration Camp. CCC for short. All the Blood Camps have some sort of reference to blood in their official designation. It was probably meant to refute a myth about vampires — that they have no sense of humor.

However, to draw a complete picture of the situation, it should be mentioned that the official designation of the camp in any of the VireArchII rankings of the Blood Camps would report the camp as CCC197. The number attached to the camp letters was assigned based on the original population of the living it had enrolled when the donation center received its first prisoners.

Perhaps the myth of no humor amongst our kind first took flight as the living noticed our preoccupation with... details.

"Nothing is too small to escape notice, as long as it is moving," is a common phrase amongst our kind.

You are alive.

We exist.

But if it does not move, it will escape our notice.

As it should.

My brethren speak of the distinct sound of the breaking of the skin of the living.

Then they subdivide their impressions depending on the age, race, and gender of those they feed on.

There are many subdivisions... within divisions... within categories, within general subject matter.

Embracing what I have become means discovering that the passage of time has changed.

After the discovery, the process of learning to deal with how time has changed is what one must embrace as well.

Winston recounted all the significant efforts of our kind who had ambitiously attempted to make the most of the one advantage that we have over the living. And though most of the stories lacked... a conclusion, all have become beacons for me as I walk this long path with the reassurance that others have gone before me.

I have found that my existence is best spent observing the world around me and then logging my findings.

What I eventually will do with these observations is not important.

Small observations. Statistics of course. Small deductions, if possible.

What is essential is to record them. Observe and record, and...

And that is all.

This existence mandate has evolved over time. And it is not something I have ever shared with my brethren.

Some would be appalled to hear of my efforts. What is the point? What is to be gained?

The answer to their veiled questions would probably only succeed in condemning me further in their eyes...

"What if I am indeed wasting my time on such pursuits? 'Time' is the only aspect of our lives where the cup runneth over."

CHAPTER FIVE

Matt woke up in the back of a military transport truck: not alone, but surrounded by at least two dozen men and women.

None of them was Jay.

His whole body ached. When he tried to sit up, a whole new level of pain kicked in and he shut his eyes.

When he opened them again, a short, pudgy, balding, middle-aged man was in his face.

"I thought you might sleep through the entire trip."

Matt tried to look away, but the pudgy, balding man simply took a few steps to his left and was right back in his grill.

"My name is Michael Leahy. You can call me 'Bunny.' That's what everyone called me at the law firm. At least they used to."

The last thing Matt wanted to do was "bond" with anyone. Certainly there was no advantage to investing in someone that looked like he would die in the first few hours of captivity.

And his military experience taught him to be wary of anyone who made a dramatic overture to become friends. There was always the chance that he was a plant from the other side.

Matt grabbed ahold of the safety net lining the walls of the truck and this time he was able to pull himself up so that he was standing.

"I know what you must be thinking, but trust me, 'Bunny' was a term of affection, nothing more."

Matt just stared at him, hoping his fixed gaze would back the man off. It didn't work. Bunny just kept talking.

"I know you're still trying to get your feet planted, but I wanted to be the first to speak to you, perhaps influence the way you'll be thinking once you start thinking clearly."

Once again Matt attempted to look past the lawyer. It was the only way to get some clues as to what happened after he and Jay were ambushed in the woods.

"I had the brilliant idea of you becoming our team leader. Think about it. If you decide to go for it, you can count on me seconding the motion. Two reasons I believe this is the right move – number one, look around... do you see any other candidates? Number two, I figure with all those dog tags hanging around your neck, you're the one with the most experience."

The dog tags around his neck were from all of the men and women who had died under his watch as an Army Ranger serving in Iraq and Afghanistan. There was a translator in Kabul who nicknamed Matt "the rapper" because of all the chains of metal hanging around his neck.

When Matt heard Bunny say, "dog tags," it prompted him to look down. Instantly he spotted the new addition to his collection. He read the name... *Jay Granville.*

Jay was dead.

The mystery of how his dog tags were now around Matt's neck is what prevented him from simply starting to cry. And his concern that Jay was really dead.

Less than a month ago the two of them were in Herndon, Virginia, walking through the burned-out wreckage of the control center of the private security firm which employed them as contracted "mercs."

Strewn all around the facility were at least fifty dead employees. Some look liked they had put up a fight, but others had self-inflicted bullet holes in their head.

"Heads up," Jay shouted to Matt before tossing him something.

It was a bullet.

"That's the one I want you to use on me. I'd tell you to do it right now, but I still believe we can beat these motherfuckers. But if the time comes, I do want you to do it. I'll feel better and you'll feel better that I'm dead… *dead*."

He was still staring at Jay's dog tags when Bunny spoke again.

"As our team leader candidate, I was hoping you could answer a question," said the chunky, hairless, weak-chinned lawyer. "Where do you think they're taking us?"

Matt needed to re-grip the netting behind him, because if he didn't, in his anger and his still shaky physical state, he would fall over once he attempted to grab Bunny by his throat.

"You need to get the fuck away from me, right now."

Bunny stumbled back, looked around to see if the others in the truck had heard what Matt had said to him, then made his way over to a corner, where he used the netting to lower himself to the floor of the truck.

The devastation of discovering Jay had died at least cleared the cobwebs in his brain. And though he was tempted to wallow in his misery, he forced himself to take a deep breath and begin thinking about the future.

Matt's eyes slowly scanned the other occupants in the truck.

There were mostly blank stares and wan faces.

Except for three females, everyone else in the cargo hold was male. The men varied in age from sixteen to senior citizens. Matt picked up enough to deduce that they came from different backgrounds, at least professionally. Executives were sitting next to construction workers. Dress shirts and slacks were side by side with T-shirts and jeans.

Matt's eyes stopped on what looked like brothers, either twins or barely a year apart. The brothers were zoning out with a single portable music player that they were sharing with two pairs of attached headphones.

He did notice that one of the females, an attractive blonde, was whispering back and forth with the men who sat on either side of her. Matt wondered if perhaps they had some plan up their sleeve.

There was the sound of screeching brakes as the truck began slowing down. In the cargo area, everyone fell into each other.

After the truck came to a complete stop, those that had been sitting used the netting to get to their feet.

Matt listened for any noises or voices coming from the outside. He was hoping to pick up on anything that might give him a clue as to what lay beyond the back of the truck.

The engine shut off.

There was the noise of footsteps running alongside the vehicle.

The military transport's back gate was unlocked, then lowered.

The canvas tarp was raised, and then thrown over the roof.

"Let's go, everyone. Double time. File out!"

The light from the setting sun caused them all to squint, but almost everyone in the cargo hold moved to comply with the order shouted out to them.

As it turned out, Matt and Bunny were the two last ones on the truck.

Before they exited, Matt grabbed ahold of Bunny's arm to get his attention.

"You can't talk your way out of this. So shut your mouth... or believe me, you're going to end up dead." The lawyer nodded his head as if he understood.

CHAPTER SIX

Even as he was hopping off the truck, Matt was focused on taking in his new environment. He was surprised to discover that he knew exactly where they were.

The truck had parked inside the main gate of an old Army training facility near his parents' farm just outside of Morristown. The place had been closed down even before he was born. He and his brother would sometimes go with their friends and mess around in some of the old buildings.

On the other side of the security checkpoint was a five-acre, fenced compound comprising a dozen 1940-era, one-story buildings. It was obvious that all the buildings had gone through a recent renovation and then splashed with a new coat of paint.

"Okay, juice boxes, immediately form a single-file line..."

The shouted order came from one of the compound guards. There were at least a dozen of them supervising their arrival. None of them looked like vampires; all were outfitted in black jumpsuits and were wielding black riot batons.

It was only after Matt stepped off the truck that he was able to see what appeared to be the only new construction in the compound – a six-story-high building, completely painted in black. It loomed over the rest of the camp like a dark specter.

As Matt moved into the line, he spotted more than a hundred male and female prisoners watching on the other side of the security-checkpoint fence.

"Last chance, juice boxes: form a line now!"

Almost all of the prisoners had originally done what they were told, but there were stragglers, even a few who felt uneasy about the situation and appeared to be making a stand.

Matt felt a whoosh of air behind him, followed by the unmistakable sound of something solid impacting human flesh. He turned to see one of his fellow prisoners had collapsed to the ground.

Standing over him was a bear of a man holding one of the riot batons. He allowed the squeal of pain coming from the prisoner to get everyone's attention before he addressed the prisoners.

"Welcome to the Coa Concentration Camp. I'm the Superintendent of Security, Ronald Spector. You won't have any trouble remembering my name because everyone remembers the name of a hero."

Spector smiled broadly as he started walking up the line of prisoners.

"Yeah, I admit I may not look like one, but believe me, I'm your hero…"

He was barrel-chested, but beyond that, Matt couldn't tell if his loose-fitting, black jumpsuit hid muscle or fat. Hearing the groans of the guy behind him did not encourage him to clarify the issue by looking directly at Spector as he walked by.

"Here's why I'm your hero – because I'm the last of the living who stands between you and...," Spector pointed his baton to the black tower, "... them."

"Growing up, my father gave me two pieces of advice. Number one – Live your life with a goal. Number two – Do whatever it takes to achieve that goal. For most of my life I ignored my father's advice, until recent worldwide events forced me to reevaluate his wise words."

Spector walked past Bunny, and the lawyer couldn't believe his luck – he recognized the head of security as one of his old clients. In fact, before the takeover he had kept his ass out of jail!

"Right now my goal is to stay alive. And I will do whatever it takes... to achieve my goal."

The head of the CCC facility had arrived right back where he had begun, standing over the prisoner he had assaulted with his baton in the gut.

Spector delivered a jackbooted kick to the prisoner's ribs. He then turned to finish his address above the moans of pain from the prisoner.

"During your stay with us, your goal is to provide services. Providing services is the only reason all of you are still alive. If you fail to provide services, you will not be achieving your goal. And when you fail to achieve your goal, you will be threatening my goal as well. Let me remind you of my earlier statement – I will do whatever it takes to achieve my goal."

This time Spector used his black baton to strike the back of the whimpering prisoner lying at his feet.

One of the other prisoners could not stand to hear the screams of pain any longer and made a move to help him.

All it took was for Spector to glare in her direction. Whatever altruistic urge the female prisoner had was squelched and she fell back into line.

"The problem with my father was that he was a... windbag," said Spector to the prisoners. "It was one of the many reasons we never got along. I heard the same two pieces of advice over and over again. The good news is none of you will have a similar problem. Everything I've just now said I will not... ever... repeat again."

Matt's gaze landed on Bunny ahead of him in line. The lawyer had a confident gleam in his eyes, as if he had just found out that he had the honor of arguing in front of the Supreme Court.

"So, let me be your hero. Follow my directions without any questions. Follow the directions of those who work with me. Let us all help you accomplish your goal."

Spector motioned to one of the compound guards.

"Okay, juice boxes, you heard the chief, proceed forward until we give you the word!"

The line surged forward toward the main camp compound.

Bunny waited until Spector was walking right beside him.

"Ron... Ron... it's me, Bunny."

At first Spector didn't seem to hear Bunny.

"Ron... over here... it's me..."

Spector finally responded, but he spoke under his breath. "Just keep it moving, juice box."

Bunny heard the words, but completely missed the subtext.

"C'mon, Ron, you gotta remember... three years ago you had that second DUI and I was able to make it go away with you just doing community service..."

Spector interrupted the lawyer with a baton blow to Bunny's back, which immediately put him down on the ground.

"I know exactly who you are, Michael Leahy, Esquire, but maybe you haven't been paying attention to who I've become..."

A voice inside Matt's head screamed for him to simply do as the other prisoners were doing ahead of him: simply walk around Bunny as if he was a pothole in the middle of the road.

But he reached down and grabbed one of Bunny's arms.

Matt glanced over to see how Spector was going to react and was surprised to see the head of security had already moved on.

His recovery took more than a few steps, but Bunny eventually started to walk on his own as they both approached a grey building.

"Thanks for the help..."

"Didn't I tell you to shut the fuck up? Next time I'll let you drown in your own vomit..."

The words were loud enough, and alarming enough, that two of the other prisoners marching nearby stepped in to relieve Matt of his burden.

He regretted his words the moment they left his mouth.

And what caused Matt the most shame were the faces of the prisoners who took over helping Bunny. They both looked at him with the same fear in their eyes that just seconds ago had been directed toward Spector.

CHAPTER SEVEN

As the newbies marched into the main compound, a young man had to hold his blue jeans by the waist or they would drop to his ankles. He had lost so much weight trying to avoid capture that his pants no longer fit. Seeing the veteran prisoners that had come to greet them, the young man shouted out, "What's in the grey building?"

His inquiry triggered an immediate reaction from one of the CCC guards, who yanked the young man out of the line, delivered several baton blows, and kicked him repeatedly. The young man squirmed in the dirt moaning in pain, next to his blue jeans which he had lost during the beating.

"It's all right. Just do what they say…," yelled Roque Juarez, one of the veteran prisoners in the CCC facility. He was a wiry and nimble-looking Hispanic who was moving in lockstep, fifty feet away but parallel to the newbies, as they made their way toward the grey building.

"Just remember one thing, everything that happens in there, stays in there."

Another veteran prisoner shouted out to them, "You've made it this far. Just stay with their program, and we'll be here when you come out." The words of encouragement came from Cliff Barrett, a broad and muscular middle-aged man who was tossing a football nervously from one hand to the other as he kept pace right behind Juarez.

A few feet away from the main entrance of the grey building, one of the CCC guards stopped the assembly of prisoners.

The building's doors opened, revealing a single, black-clad, concentration-camp guard standing in the doorway. He waved to the first prisoner in line as if he was a barker working the sidewalk in front of a strip joint.

"Right this way. Everything is going to be great…"

While all the prisoners were filing into the room, Matt had some time to assess what lay ahead. The room they were standing in was large and well lit, but Matt estimated it to be less than a fourth of the entire building. An observation room, encased entirely in dark glass, had been constructed in the rafters. No doubt it was where new arrivals could be evaluated.

When the last of the newbies entered the grey building, a CCC guard shut the door behind him.

Immediately a noise coming from the front of the room grabbed their attention. Another CCC guard slid open the wall, revealing an even larger area beyond where they were all standing. What lay on the other side was impossible to fathom, because the entire area was engulfed in a cloud of steam.

A physical altercation suddenly broke out near Matt. He turned to see that one of the male prisoners was being restrained by another, as a thin, pasty-faced woman with blonde hair moved away from them.

She moved with confidence through the group, despite the fact that a few of the prisoners shook their heads in disgust. The blonde took a place reserved for her, right next to the CCC guard who had revealed the fake wall.

"You will strip off all of your clothes and your personal possessions and leave them in a pile beside you."

Matt remembered seeing her on the truck, talking to two male prisoners. She had looked emaciated, like she hadn't eaten in days. He also noticed red scratches on her neck. Only now did he realize how he had created the blonde woman's backstory without speaking one word to her. It was clearly what the vampires were counting on.

"Your personal possessions will be returned to you. This is an opportunity for all of you to experience how much you can trust us when you follow our directions. However, if you choose to ignore our directives, the next stage of orientation will be very challenging. Any transgressions will result in a punishment. The penalty for your transgression might even result in your death. Now, as I have previously instructed, remove all of your clothing."

There was silence.

Then four of the prisoners started to take off their clothes.

Everyone in the room turned, some had sneers on their face; others began to cry while most just looked confused as to what they should do.

An African-American prisoner standing in front of the four disrobing prisoners shoved his nearly naked comrade.

A CCC guard standing nearby used his baton to strike the African American across his leg.

Almost as a group, the four naked prisoners, stepped over the injured African American and headed to the front of the room.

"Very good," said the blonde informer. "Now walk through to the other side and discover that your obedience will be rewarded with a slice of cake on the other side."

One by one the four prisoners walked through the wall and into the thick cloud of mist.

"The cake is not a lie. And I will offer the next five who do as they have been instructed the same reward. All the rest of you will miss out on the cake and, more importantly, you threaten your very existence."

At that point, most of the other prisoners began to disrobe.

And very quickly it also became a race as several of the prisoners tore off their clothes, hoping to be one of the five who would get cake on the other side.

As several prisoners rushed toward the open wall, one was stopped by the blonde informer. She motioned to her fellow guards and the man was taken away, through the open wall, but in a different direction than the prisoners who had preceded him.

Matt recognized the prisoner who had been taken away as someone who had been sitting and conversing with the female plant during the truck ride to the concentration camp.

"That concludes the offer of a reward for your cooperation," the blonde female plant announced. "The rest of you now have exactly three minutes to achieve your goal or suffer the consequences."

Everyone else that was still in the room quickly began taking off their clothes.

After they left the grey building's initiation room, Matt and the other prisoners were divided into groups of six, then led underneath showers where they were sprayed with different streams of colored water – red, then blue, and finally green.

Whatever chemical was "blue," it stung like a hot iron on Matt's skin.

Several of the prisoners tried to step away when they were hit with the blue water. CCC guards were standing nearby, waving batons, and chasing the prisoners back until all of the prisoners had been sprayed.

Still dripping wet, the groups of six were then funneled into three separated lines. There they waited to be individually examined by a doctor.

Matt checked out all of the three doctors performing the examinations, and none were wearing the black uniforms like the rest of the CCC guards.

When he was called to step forward for his medical check-up he was greeted by an older man, with short cropped white hair and beard, who looked to be making his best effort to appear cheerful.

"My name is Dr. Garrett Dietz. Why don't we start with your…?"

But the moment Dietz reached out, Matt stopped him, grabbing the doctor by the wrist.

"It appears we can skip the tests regarding your reflexes. But we'll still need to measure your blood pressure…"

"How can you work for these animals…?"

"Just like you… I want to stay alive."

"Is that the only excuse you have?"

"No, but it's the one that's usually acceptable in most situations."

He tightened his grip on the doctor's wrist.

"Listen to me, you either let me examine you… or I will be doing your autopsy later. Autopsies are so much more work."

"What's in it for me?" asked Matt.

"You live."

Matt audibly scoffed at Dietz's words.

"Why would they go to all the trouble to bring you here… just to kill you?" asked Dietz. "Killing you is the last thing they want."

"I hope you're not talking about me becoming one of them?"

"No, they don't want that either."

He still wasn't sure and refused to release the doctor's wrist.

Dietz nodded toward the glass-encased wall above them.

"If you don't let me go, in about ten seconds, maybe less, the guards will be here to make sure you do. And there's no telling what will happen to you after that…"

Matt finally let go of the doctor's wrist.

Dietz began checking his blood pressure.

Then he stuck a needle into Matt's arm, extracting some blood. He read the digital summary and raised an eyebrow.

"AB negative. The rarest blood type. I'm betting you already knew that..."

The doctor performed some more tests and then motioned for Matt to proceed.

"Now what happens?"

"I'm not allowed to spoil the surprise. But I will see you on the other side."

Still naked, Matt and the other prisoners were led to the largest area in the building. In a single-file line, they were spaced out until each of them stood in front of their own small, empty room.

Over a loudspeaker came the voice of one of the CCC guards.

"When you hear the whistle, you are to step forward and enter the stall in front of you."

The sound of a whistle was piped over the loudspeaker.

Most of the prisoners did exactly as they were told and entered their individual holding pen.

A few of the newbies ignored the sound and stood in place.

Matt was one of those reluctant to move forward.

One of the CCC guards rushed up and shoved a baton into his back, which sent him sprawling headfirst into his stall. The access door slammed shut behind him.

Matt stood up and looked around his pen. Even in almost pitch blackness, he could see that the walls, like the floor, were solid concrete. But there was no ceiling. He could see all the way to the top of the building, which had been made of glass. Matt could see that it was now nighttime outside.

There was a loud voice from a few stalls away. "You go to hell! I'm a lawyer for Christ's sakes! You can't treat me like this!"

Matt had no trouble recognizing Bunny's voice… or the unmistakable noise of several baton blows to his body.

Eventually, the screams from Bunny and the other resisting prisoners fell silent.

One of the concrete walls in Matt's holding pen slowly rumbled open, revealing a completely pitch-black void on the other side. Whatever rays of moonlight were streaming through the glass ceiling were not shining on the other side of the stall opening.

Just as Matt decided to brace himself for the worse, three shadows streaked across the stall. He managed to throw a kick in the direction of the shadows, but that only made it easier for him to be taken down when his head slammed against the solid concrete.

Pain from the impact radiated through his body.

He then felt a jabbing sting coming from his throat and wrist.

His reaction was silenced before it could emerge from his mouth.

Then all of the pain that had been shooting through his body was silenced as well.

From that point on, Matt felt disconnected from his body.

He was still aware of what was happening, but it was as if his head had been severed from his body, and was floating above the pen like a balloon, allowing him to see the rest of his body being assaulted by three vampires.

CHAPTER EIGHT

Once again Matt had a grip on Dr. Dietz's wrist.

"You need this shot."

"Like I needed three vampires draining me of my blood?!"

"The alternative was your execution... and maybe mine."

"I guess the sanctity of the patient-doctor relationship was a casualty of the takeover."

"I didn't lie to you. You're alive... and you're not one of them. Taking your blood and turning you are two different processes."

Matt finally let go of Dietz's wrist.

The doctor had to wiggle his fingers to get some feeling back.

As soon as he felt the sensitivity returning, Dietz plunged the needle into Matt's bicep and injected a B-vitamin supplement.

"If it makes you feel any better, what you went through won't be repeated. The experience was meant to make you more compliant the next time you donate blood."

Matt just stared at him without responding.

Dietz grabbed one of the Blood Donation Center's "welcome packages." It contained a towel, a wash cloth, an orange jumpsuit, and small toiletry kit that included soap, toothpaste/toothbrush, and deodorant.

The doctor set the package at Matt's feet.

"Okay, so you've been a great audience. I play in this lounge every week, but I'm hoping that the two pint cover charge will discourage you from ever coming again..."

Then he left Matt alone in the stall to change into his new clothes.

"Shit!"

It was hard to believe that Tyra Redmond still felt the jolt of pain when something sharp penetrated her skin.

"What the hell are you doing?"

"Sorry about that, Tyra. Still trying to get the hang of this new needle."

Tyra had twenty-six different tattoos covering her chest, arms, and neck. Her upper body had become what she called a "tatimony" to her run-ins with the vampires. Every pair of fang marks got their own tattoo, each one carved around the incisor scars.

Just a few days ago Tyra was caught with a shank by one of the goons. She was immediately taken to the grey building, where that night she acquired another pair of fang marks to go with the others.

Her latest tattoo was a spider carved around the vampire tracks.

Ralph, the CCC prison tat artist, was an aging hippie snatched three months ago on one of the patrol sweeps. He once had his own tat shop in Venice, California, but had given up the trade over twenty years ago. Now he was doing what he could, utilizing his skills as a tattoo artist so that the other prisoners of the camp wouldn't see him as a weak link.

Tyra used her index finger to swipe up the blood oozing from the cut on her arm. She was about to wipe it on her jumpsuit, but it suddenly occurred to her, that after more than six months of captivity, not once had she tasted her own blood.

She swished it around her mouth like her father used to do while tasting fine wine.

Then Tyra spit it out.

"I hear it's an acquired taste," said Ralph.

The doors to the grey building flew open.

Tyra immediately stood and watched as the camp newbies began filing out.

"Waiting for someone?"

She didn't answer him. Tyra liked Ralph, but other than the fact that he had carved almost a dozen tattoos on her body, she didn't know anything about him.

"Got a rag on you?"

Ralph gave her the wash cloth in his pocket. She used it to wipe off the blood as she continued to stare across the compound.

The guy Tyra was looking for emerged from the grey building. He was almost one of the last prisoners to exit before one of the goons closed the door behind them.

She started off in the direction of the "juice stand"; the table the goons had set up to offer orange juice to all the newbies.

"Tyra… my rag," Ralph called after her.

She stopped and looked at her tattoo. The spider only had four legs.

"I'll be back later to get the other half of my tattoo." She then tossed Ralph his rag.

Matt was in the middle of downing a plastic cup of orange juice when he heard a voice that seemed to be directed toward him.

"I know you, right?"

After he had drained the juice from the plastic cup, Matt looked over to see a woman, about thirty years old, staring at him. Like all the veteran prisoners, she appeared to be alert and adequately fed.

He threw the empty cup in a trash can but didn't say anything to Tyra as he walked right past her.

Tyra shook her head, and followed after him.

"Yeah, you're definitely the guy in the Green Zone that night. You were working for the Frontline Security Firm, right?"

Matt not only stopped walking, he turned, then took a step toward her.

"What did one of my colleagues do? Steal a Humvee? Fuck one of your translators? Look I wish I could help, but I'm not responsible for any of the assholes I worked with back in the Green Zone. Especially not now."

He was off again, as if their conversation was finished.

Once again, Tyra followed after him.

"So you don't remember being at the McAlister International hotel?"

"Sorry, I don't," replied Matt.

His response was too quick for Tyra, as if he had taken no time to think about it.

"You just donated two pints of blood, perhaps that could have impaired your memory?"

"Sorry. Not ringing a bell."

Despite his answer, she kept walking with him. After several seconds of silence, her persistence eventually triggered another response from him.

"I was drinking a lot while working for FSF. That could have something to do with it."

"Those of us who worked in the State Department used to say that the letters FSF stood for 'Fuck you, Stop looking at me, we don't Fucking work for the military'."

"I guess the State Department doesn't make it a priority to brief their employees on the use of acronyms..."

"Perhaps you're right. But they do allow us to attend parties put on by private security firms like FSF. That's how I wound up meeting you in the basement of the McAlister hotel."

Matt stopped walking and looked at her.

"We were doing vodka shots...?"

"That's right..." Tyra tried to smile, but she was sure her effort was similar to what she looked like as a teenager when her parents tried to take a picture of her.

"So it's all coming back to you?"

This time he looked like he was making a real effort to recall more details.

"Nope. Drawing a blank after the vodka shots. What did I do; skip out on the bill?"

"There was no bill. It was a party."

He thought some more, but eventually just shook his head.

"Around midnight you got this call from your mobile phone. After you hung up you took one more shot, then said something about 'your package' being on the move and… you needed to leave."

She revealed her words gradually, like she was providing clues to someone suffering from amnesia and that any clue might trigger total recall of the event.

"Yeah, right… I needed to leave," he said. "Now I remember: the 'package' was the Vice President of the United States. The phone call came from the point man on the security detail with a change of plans. The VP needed to fly back to the States that instant because…" It was there his memory came to an abrupt halt. Matt wasn't surprised. He never gave a shit about such details.

He started walking again. "Look, whatever reason the client had to leave, it meant I had to leave. It was my job."

"Just so you know, while you were jetting around on Air Force Two with the Vice President, I stayed behind in the Green Zone. That was my home for the next three years, dodging mortar attacks and insurgent bombs."

"Sounds horrific. Thank god you received the appreciation from a grateful nation," said Matt.

"Yeah, it was a real victory parade. For weeks I was removing confetti that had lodged underneath my nails."

He stopped walking. The last thing he wanted after being sucked dry by three vampires was some government employee yammering on about how bad things had gotten in Iraq.

Like he hadn't been there.

Like he hadn't experienced some of his men getting killed there.

"I'm sorry, I didn't catch your name…?"

"Tyra."

"Tyra, in case you didn't notice, it's the end of the world. Why don't we pick up this conversation the next time we're both standing in the basement of the McAlister hotel?"

"That would be great. Except that the hotel is gone. Along with everything else in the Green Zone."

He looked away. Took a deep breath, then turned back to her.

"Why don't you spill whatever you've got to say about what I've done."

"You took my last pack of smokes."

He looked around the compound as if their whole discussion was being shot by hidden cameras. "Is this like some vampire reality show and I'm being jerked for more than just my blood?"

She was not deterred by his reaction.

"When you fled the party at the McAlister hotel, you asked for a cigarette, and you ended up taking the entire pack. Taking someone's last pack of cigarettes in the middle of a war zone is a fucked-up thing to do."

He started to respond, but instead shook his head and started walking again.

"Maybe if you were a real soldier you'd understand what you did."

He stopped immediately and wheeled around to respond –

"I did two tours as an Army Ranger. One in Iraq and the other in Afghanistan."

"My father and my brother were both Marines."

"Really? Marines? Impressive. Where's your father now? Your brother?"

Her face froze and the color drained away.

Matt was instantly ashamed of what he said. But instead of admitting his mistake, he started walking again.

This time she did not follow.

With every step he took, his words continued to play back in his head like an endless audio loop. He stopped walking and turned back around.

"That was... wrong... disrespectful... what I said."

Before Tyra could respond he started walking again.

Tyra needed to almost run to catch up with him.

"Where did the bloodsuckers track you down?"

He wasn't excited that she had decided to continue the conversation, but he was relieved that she had let go of his remarks about her father and brother.

"Not far from here. I was checking out my ex-wife's house when one of the blood patrols cornered me."

"Why in the world would you be checking up on your ex-wife?"

He shook his head and refused to respond, but his response to her question came at the exact time they were walking past a CCC guard, and the goon interpreted Matt's impatience with Tyra.

"Were you just now eyeballin' me, juice box?"

Matt knew enough to stop walking, cast his eyes to the ground, and look contrite before responding.

"I was not looking at you disrespectfully, sir. I apologize. It won't happen again."

Satisfied with his reaction, the CCC guard resumed his patrol.

The two resumed their walk across the compound.

"So who made those guys boss?"

"The vampires. Those sellouts manage our entire day, making sure the blood donation twice a week goes well. Then at night the goons turn things over to the vampires."

They had arrived at the prisoners' barracks building.

Matt tried to enter, but before he could even grab the handle, she stepped between him and the door.

"It appears the greedy-dick chip embedded in your hard drive is still fully functioning. But I'll be honest with you; I believe our only realistic hope is to rely on guys… like you. Almost everyone has been in this place for at least three months; most have been here twice as long. That's why I've decided to go 'all in' and bet that you're still capable of being a 'team player' and will be someone who could help us with a plan to escape."

Tyra concluded her pitch by extending her hand toward the newbie.

"That was a hell of a recruitment speech. For the record, you had me at 'greedy' and 'dick,' but you lost me at 'team player'."

The thought of using her hand to strike the asshole across the face crossed Tyra's mind before she simply lowered it.

"To be honest with you, I only have two items on my 'to do' list – grab a bunk, and keep to myself."

She stood there staring at him, shaking her head.

"And by the way, you got a lot of blood dripping from you neck. I'd take care of that before the sun sets."

Tyra slapped her hand up to her half-tattoo.

He motioned to the door.

She stepped aside and let the newbie enter the building.

CHAPTER NINE

The moment Matt stepped through the barracks door, a football was spiraling toward his head. It would have hit him square in the forehead if Juarez had not snatched the football out of the air just a few inches from Matt's face.

"Nice throw, jackass," Juarez shouted out to whoever had thrown the pass before turning around to address Matt.

"Sorry about that. Not exactly how we want to greet any of the new prisoners."

"No problem," Matt answered, without looking at Juarez. He was more interested in the rest of the building.

The man who had tossed the football had enough manners to come over and apologize for almost causing an injury. "Wow! Almost got you with that one," said Barrett. "I'm blaming the elbow I injured in high school for that lousy pass…"

"No problem," answered Matt.

Juarez laughed. "Is that the only two words you know?"

"I also know, 'where is the john?' 'where do we get our food,' 'fuck you.' And 'leave me the fuck alone'. And I know all those phrases in eleven different languages."

Then, without another word, Matt stepped around Barrett and Juarez to check out the rest of the building.

"Was it the way I smelled?" asked Barrett as soon as Matt was out of earshot.

"No, I think it's the way we all smell," Juarez shot back.

"This is the guy I was telling you about. He was working for this private security firm, and just like the company, the guy was a dick."

"Looks like he still is a dick," said Juarez.

"That's not fair. Didn't you think I was a dick when you first met me?" said Barrett.

"No, I thought you were a pussy," said Juarez, as he started jogging away. "I'm going long. Hit me…"

Barrett rolled out with the football, leaving Tyra standing by herself.

At first she thought that the rough exterior he displayed could have been triggered by the fact she was a woman. But after seeing him deal with Juarez and Cliff, she realized Matt clearly had some personal issues.

And yet as she watched him moving through the barracks, she had the hope that there was room to navigate between the wall Matt had put up and the personal experiences that might have damaged his psyche along the way.

But then, Tyra thought to herself, she was probably just fooling herself.

Matt walked slowly and deliberately down the middle aisle of the barracks. Instantly the conditions reminded him of the overcrowded facility in Kabul where they held captured terrorists and the locals they suspected of cooperating with the Taliban.

Bunk was upon bunk, and just inches apart from the next tower of bunks, starting just ten feet from the main entrance to the farthest wall.

Though he appeared to keep his eyes staring forward, he caught snatches through his peripheral vision of the other prisoners. His goal was not to learn something about them, but to make sure they didn't get the wrong impression of who he was. He wanted to look determined, not insecure, as he searched for a bunk vacancy. Everyone around him, now all staring at him... had somehow survived the takeover. He didn't want to play into any of the factors that might explain why they had all survived while everyone else had died.

Matt had almost reached the other side of the building when he saw what looked like an empty top bunk. On the bottom bunk was a man reading a book, so Matt couldn't see his face at first.

He could see some photos taped to the footlocker below the bunk. Photos of a middle-aged, white guy holding a sniper rifle as if it was a fishing rod. There were also magazine cutouts of Kennedy, King, and Gandhi. Below the montage were the crudely carved words, "Happiness is a cold bullet."

"Excuse me... can I help you?"

"Not unless you plan on putting a mint on my pillow."

Matt didn't wait for a reaction as he leaped up on to the top bunk and reclined like the only thing he was waiting for was a cold beer.

His new bunkmate was named Lincoln Grouse, and he swung his legs out from his bed and stood up with some urgency. He tried his best not to come off as if he was worried, but there was no doubt that Grouse was bothered by Matt's sudden intrusion into his space.

"Who decided this?"

Matt looked over, but because Grouse wasn't especially tall, it meant his beady eyes were several inches below the level of the top bunk.

"You're looking at him."

"Really? Well, then you should know the bed you're sleeping on comes with some history. The previous occupant was a guy named Mendelsohn, a real fat fuck who died in his sleep. His last moments were spent right there, where you're lying now."

He raised himself up on an elbow, pretending he really cared to hear more.

"You're saying he died right here?"

"Yeah, that's what I'm telling you. Three weeks ago he begged to be delivered from the hell he was suffering on Earth. So I smothered him…"

Matt punched the pillow beneath his head.

"With this very pillow…?"

"Yeah, with that very pillow…" Lincoln Grouse then nodded solemnly. "Praise God."

"Well, you should know, I have my own shameful history… of smothering my fellow bunkmates… with a pillow just like this. I got away with the first incident, but the Rangers discharged me when it happened a second time. "

Grouse did his best to stand his ground, and not react to anything he had heard. But the look in Matt's face scared the shit out of him.

Not that he got a real long look. Anytime anyone looked straight at Lincoln and maintained their stare, just as Matt was now doing, Grouse would look away, completely intimidated.

Without another word, Lincoln Grouse silently descended out of Matt's view like he was the setting sun.

The moment his bunkmate was out of eyesight, Matt sat up.

The other newbies had already started to enter the building.

At least Tyra had been waiting for him.

There didn't appear to be anyone waiting to greet the others.

Looking around he could see why. Something along the lines of what Tyra had said. Everyone who had been there for months probably were afraid that the newbies were there to replace them.

.

CHAPTER TEN

"I'm coming for you… hang in there…"

Ian was crawling along the main beam that stretched across the barn toward his brother. Matt's fingertips were white and turning purple as they struggled to hold onto the same beam.

"Did you hear me, Matty? I'm almost there…"

He could feel his strength draining away. He knew he had to try one more time to pull himself up. Matt summoned everything left and tried to swing his legs forward to give himself some momentum… but the effort only made him finally lose his grip on the beam.

He was falling.

Out of nowhere, his brother's hand locked on to his wrist.

"Got you…!"

Matt woke up.

He did not know where he was.

Finally his heavy breathing gave way to the sound of the breathing, coughing, and snoring of hundreds of men and women sleeping around him.

It was the middle of the night and he was surprised, and a bit uneasy, by how deeply he slept… considering the circumstances.

He couldn't believe that he had a dream about his brother. It had been years since his brother appeared in one of his dreams.

Matt closed his eyes.

Instantly, Ian's face popped into his mind's eye. The image of his brother seemed to grow more intense, as if it was burning into his retinas.

Matt flashed open his eyes.

He was shocked to discover he was no longer in his bunk, but standing in the center aisle of the barracks building. Before he could contemplate how he had somehow left his bunk, Matt saw movement in the center of the room.

A figure moved past the rows of bunk beds toward the building exit. His eyes scanned the room to see who else was awake and might have seen the apparition.

But all the prisoners in the building were fast asleep.

The image of his brother Ian popped into his head. Why would he be dreaming of Ian when his brother had been dead for years?

He didn't have the answer, but the image of his brother seemed to burn with such intensity that he felt compelled to stumble forward to relieve the pain.

There was a chill in the air as Matt suddenly realized he was standing outside the door of the barracks building. He looked up and saw huge search lights mounted on the concentration-camp towers.

Then all the lights switched off.

Only the light from a quarter moon was left behind, or Matt would be struggling to see in total darkness.

"Matt…"

It was not a whisper, nor was the voice something he heard in his head. Something in between.

"I'm coming for you Matty…"

The next noise came from above, and he looked up in enough time to see a dark shadow descending toward him. Rather than moving away, Matt felt compelled to raise his right arm. He stretched his fingers as if they were trying to touch the sky.

"Got you…!"

Suddenly his feet were off the ground… and Matt was floating toward the night sky. The stars and the moon were getting closer and closer, then the freezing hand released him and he fell a short distance to the gravel covering the rooftop of the barracks building.

It took him a few seconds to orientate himself, though there was a part of Matt that was convinced what was happening was just the continuation of his earlier dream.

"Matty…"

The shadowy cloud that had caused him to rise from the ground to the roof was gone. But the nighttime sky was all around him, along with the stars and the moon. And there was something else, he could feel it.

"Is that you…? Answer me… Ian…?"

A hand covered his mouth.

"Shh…"

It was the same frost-cold hand that had held his wrist. His lips immediately turned numb and a freezing burn radiated all across his face.

"No one can know about this…"

Just as he was about to scream in pain, he was released.

The blood rushed back to his skin as he touched his lips and the rest of his face. The feeling of frostbite was either imaginary or transitory.

"It's me, Matty…"

He turned toward the voice. A figure stood in the shadows near the rooftop entrance. Matt shook his head… one last attempt to wake himself, if indeed what was happening was part of a dream.

"Ian? It can't be you… you're…"

"… dead."

There was a dim light shining above the rooftop exit door, which cast an umbrella of soft light. Ian stepped out of the shadows so his brother could see for the first time what he had become.

"I know, Matty, not a pretty sight."

It was clearly Ian's voice, even though the words were coming from something that resembled a corpse.

"But isn't your reaction to my appearance shocking only because it's in conflict with your past memory of what I once looked like?"

"No, my reaction is because you're dead."

The content, the immediacy, and the decisiveness of his brother's answer drove Ian back into the rooftop shadows.

"Mom… Dad… we all thought… because you had simply disappeared, that you had been taken by a serial killer."

"Matt, that's not too far from the truth."

Now his voice seemed to come from a different part of the roof. Matt narrowed his eyes and realized that the figure standing in the shadows was no longer standing there.

"If you want to classify the vampire that turned you... a serial killer," said Matt, "I certainly won't disagree with you. But it's not the fate any of us imagined for you."

"Yes, of course. Forgive me. I'm sorry to be so disconnected with what you went through. You must understand, the ten years since my disappearance feels like another lifetime ago."

Matt still couldn't see Ian, and his brother's slight, wispy voice seemed to be floating all around him in the air. He decided to simply stare into the dark space in front of him and speak.

"Well, perhaps it's been another life for you, but I was involved in the one you had with Mom and Dad. You should know that both of them went to their graves believing the worst about how you had died."

Ian was suddenly standing right next to him.

"You really need to lower your voice…"

He was so close, Matt could smell his breath. It smelled like zinc.

"Does what Mom and Dad went through mean anything to you?"

"Yes, of course. But don't you think it was better they saw my face on a milk carton and wept for me... rather than learn the truth – that I was one of those responsible for the disappearance of the other faces on the same milk cartons?"

Matt stepped away from his brother. His mind was racing. A decade ago, when he thought Ian had died at the hands of some killer, he thought obsessively about all the things he wished he had told his brother. Now he couldn't remember one word.

"I knew you would show up at Beth's house, if you were still alive," said Ian. "After I was assigned to this facility I planted video cameras there."

"Then you would know if..."

Matt could not finish his sentence; Ian's hand was once again over his mouth. In his anxiousness, Matt was practically yelling out his question.

"Last time, Matty..."

He nodded.

When Ian released him, Matt whispered his question. "Is Beth alive?"

"I was not assigned to the facility until months after the takeover. By that time Beth was already gone... or killed. Her name has not turned up on any of the donation center rosters on the eastern corridor. That's all I know."

His next question was louder than a whisper. In his anger it was the best he could do.

"So you killed Jay?"

"I tried to allow for every possible contingency, but I failed. I assure you, your friend's death was in no way part of my plan. I hope you believe me."

Matt turned toward the voice, and was startled to discover his brother was standing right beside him. And somehow he was holding Jay's dog tags, which had just been around his neck.

"I saw the other chains around your neck. It made sense to add your friend's chain as well. If I made the wrong choice... forgive me."

Matt closed his eyes, trying to control his temper.

He opened them when he felt Jay's chain drop back around his neck. But Ian was no longer standing near him.

"Your well-being continues to be a primary importance in my life. Don't think I haven't watched over you all these years. Checked to see how my little brother was progressing."

Once again, Ian's voice seemed to be disembodied words floating through the night air.

"That's beautiful," said Matt. "My own guardian angel."

Suddenly, Ian was right next to him again.

"Perhaps if you knew how true those words were you would choose a more appreciative way to express them."

He was processing what Ian was saying, and not able to immediately respond.

"Matty, we have been hiding amongst you for thousands and thousands of years. Certainly when I was turned, I did so for a reason. All these years I have spent a considerable amount of time existing… just a shadow away from you."

"I have no idea what you're talking about," said Matt.

"Sure you do. Come on, my brother, what did you think? All this time, you've managed to stay alive because you've been… 'lucky'?"

He had heard enough. Matt turned and started to move away, but cold fingers grabbed his shoulder and turned him back around.

"This is not how I wanted our reunion to go."

Matt looked shell-shocked as he stared at Ian. Everything about the last ten years, his memories, core beliefs, all of it was now up for grabs.

"Don't hide from this. Go over everything in your mind, Matty. When you do, I know you'll see the truth. I have no regrets. You, on the other hand should be questioning some of the choices you've made. Don't add to your mistakes…"

He had nothing to say and tried to move away again. But when Matt threw open the roof's exit door, Ian was standing on the other side.

Matt tried to move past him. Ian was disappointed by his brother's action.

"Do what you will, Matty, but no one can know about our connection…"

The rooftop door slammed behind Ian, and that's how Matt knew they were moving backwards with his brother's hand wrapped around his throat.

"Obviously you don't appreciate what I tried to do for you, but there are those amongst my kind who will still use my effort against me…"

Matt tried to swing at his brother, but Ian's bony fingers dug deeper into his neck.

"If you would only trust me… like when we were kids…"

Nothing Matt was screaming inside his head was emerging from his lips.

"The two of us… together… Matty… we can survive all of this…"

Matt flashed his eyes open with a start.

He was back in his bunk staring up at the ceiling.

The first rays of the morning sun were starting to light up the steel beams above him.

Sitting up, he saw some of the other prisoners were still asleep, but others were moving around.

Many thoughts were running through his head. He wasn't sure about any of them.

Then he saw purple bruise marks on his wrist. He checked his other arm and discovered the same. Matt pulled up the collar on his neck and lay down. He had not been dreaming.

The nightmare he had been living for most of his life had just started another chapter.

CHAPTER ELEVEN

The rising sun wasn't yet visible as the prisoners hopped out of their beds and scrambled to get their clothes and shoes on.

This was the first morning for the newbies in the camp, so some of the veteran prisoners took it upon themselves to push the recent arrivals through the process.

Every morning started with a loud alarm in the barracks. It was followed seconds later by the goons moving through the barracks and making sure the prisoners assembled in a timely manner at the center of the main compound.

The prisoners were supposed to assemble in lines of eleven prisoners each. But Juarez and Barrett would intentionally screw with the guards by making sure none of the lines ever contained exactly eleven people.

It was one of the reasons the goons did both a roll call and a head count.

However, even Juarez and Barrett wouldn't dare downplay the importance the goons placed on their two daily roll calls -- the one in the morning, and the other in the early evening. The times for the two roll calls changed all the time, probably as a security strategy. But the second roll call always occurred before dark.

The first of three meals was served two hours after the first roll call. The kitchen was manned by prisoners, supervised by camp guards.

The vampires knew enough about the living to know that their prisoners wouldn't eat heartily if they didn't trust who was cooking their meals.

Matt had some vegetable soup ladled into his bowl. Another prisoner, wearing an apron over his camp fatigues, next dished out three slices of Spam onto Matt's plate. For breakfast.

"This is the way the world ends, not with a bang… but with soup and Spam."

It was Juarez paraphrasing T.S. Elliot.

Matt was not in the mood to be amused, and tried to keep on moving forward, but that was when he realized Barrett, Juarez's straight man, was standing in front of him.

"My pal back there is a poet… and I didn't even know it," said Barrett.

"How can you look forward to three meals a day when all of it is crap?" said Juarez.

When Matt didn't respond, Juarez used his tray to tap him on the shoulder.

"Wanna know what's for lunch?" asked Juarez.

Matt wouldn't respond.

"Barrett, tell the new recruit…"

"Sugar sandwiches."

"He's not fucking joking."

"I heard through the camp grapevine the bloodsuckers have trademarked the recipe," said Barrett.

"That might explain why we've eaten it every single day since we've been here," shouted Juarez. He shoved his tray into Matt's back. "Wanna know the secret recipe for 'sugar sandwiches'? Tell him Barrett…"

"Lots of butter spread over white bread and then covered with sugar," Barrett answered without missing a beat.

"Yum, yum, right?"

Matt got his drink and left the line for a table.

It didn't stop Juarez from talking. He just directed his comedy routine toward one of the goons standing nearby, supervising the meal.

"Somebody should tell the bloodsuckers that we might taste better if they didn't keep feeding us sugar sandwiches and pig anus!"

"Hold on there, partner, Spam is not pig anus," protested Barrett. "My stepbrother grew up in Hawaii, and there's no way he would eat pig anus every day and still be able to say 'aloha'."

Whatever Juarez's retort was, Matt didn't hear it. He quickly made his way across the mess hall to the first empty table.

After a few bites, he raised his eyes to look around the enormous mess hall.

There were a lot of tables, but not many people. Were there other mess halls? For the first time, Matt started to realize that perhaps the crowded barracks building was just one of the buildings in the compound.

As he ate his meal, Matt made it a point to take in the sights of the other prisoners sitting around him.

The twin brothers were eating together… still sharing an iPod while they ate their breakfast.

Dietz was just a couple of tables away, sitting by himself. Matt watched as the doctor waited for both of the supervising goons to look the other way before pouring some green liquid into his coffee. After he stirred the cup with a spoon, he tasted it, then scribbled his reaction on a ledger next to his tray.

Sitting nearby was Matt's new bunkmate. He looked even more creepy in broad daylight than at night. Grouse had a tray of food in front of him but wasn't actually eating, just mumbling to himself as he stared at his food with disdain.

"There he is, the man of the hour…"

Tyra's attempt at a sing-song greeting came from several tables away as she got up and began carrying her tray of food toward his table. Three middle-aged, white guys, also toting trays of food, followed right behind her.

"So what's the verdict, Matt? In your opinion does the concentration camp's mess hall deserve its recent 'Michelin' star?"

Her attempt at humor was simultaneous to her grabbing a place on the bench right next to him.

Matt reacted to Tyra's joke and her unilateral decision to sit beside by staring into space. His silence froze the three men who had accompanied Tyra, and it prompted her to pick up the conversation.

"Gentlemen, don't be turned off. Sometimes the silent have the most to say. I assure you, the man I sit next to could be the key to your…"

Tyra lowered her voice to a whisper.

"…freedom."

One of the men held out his hand to Matt.

"Great to meet you. My name is Erik Chast. These are my buddies, Pete Tulliver and Rory Murphy. We all worked in the same financial-planning office together."

"Before the takeover," Tulliver chimed in after Chast had finished speaking.

Chast finally realized that Matt was not going to shake his hand and he lowered it.

"I warned you, didn't I? He's either a germaphobe... or cracking through his shell will be half the fun...?"

He turned to her with a blank stare. Matt wanted her to know that what he had said to her yesterday still stood. But all he got back from Tyra was a smile that made her look like a village idiot. Perhaps some of the bombs that had gone off in the Green Zone had caused some brain damage.

"Ty tells us you're smart and could be a real asset to our plan."

Matt looked over and saw that all three of the guys tagging along had found their seats on the bench opposite him.

He just looked hard at each one, down the line, then turned his attention back to his soup and Spam.

"I thought you said this guy could help us," said Chast.

"I said 'could' help you. There's an abyss between the words 'could' and 'would'."

"Great, we're fighting for our lives," said Murphy, "and we're carving out time for a grammar lesson."

Both Chast and Tulliver turned to Murphy with irritated looks, as if what he had said was completely out of line.

Tyra kept her focus on Matt, still watching him carefully for anything that might help her figure out how she could get through to him.

"Even though Matt has spent two tours of duty serving his country, I know he has some problems right now helping others. Do you mind, Matt, sharing with my fellow prisoners a clue as to what your objections are?"

He chewed the Spam in his mouth very slowly before answering.

"Team jerseys."

"Is that supposed to be profound?" asked Murphy.

"That's it exactly," said Tyra. "Yin and yang, right Matt? You're looking for a balance, but right now pretty much all you've experienced to date is the rest of humanity fucking you over."

He stopped chewing and turned to look at Tyra.

"Compared to what these ruthless bloodsuckers have done to us," said Chast, "I can't believe that's the way you feel about things."

"I agree," Tulliver chimed in. "Hasn't it been the vampires behaving like total assholes during this takeover? We should be shoving their yin into their yang if you get my drift."

She turned to address Chast. "Wait, I don't understand. Correct me if I'm wrong, but weren't all these asshole vampires part of 'humanity' before they became the undead?"

Tulliver looked over at Chast for help in dealing with Tyra's point.

When she was greeted with silence, Tyra tried to clarify. "The fact that they all were once human, means that what they've been doing to all of us is probably still an indictment on humanity as a whole… don't you think?"

As Tulliver and Chast were taking their time to process Tyra's words, Murphy became frustrated.

"If I had known we were meeting for breakfast to discuss philosophy, I would have brought my incense sticks…?"

"What is your problem?" Chast asked Murphy.

"Yeah, Murph, you just need to relax," said Tulliver.

"I'll relax… as soon as we actually start talking about something related to our escape plan."

"Look, Matt, the three of us are obviously jacked up," said Tulliver. "As you just heard, we're planning on breaking out of this dump. I have no idea who you are… or what your beef is… but Tyra brought us to you because we need help."

"'Need help' might be overstating the situation," Chast interrupted.

Tulliver quickly turned to his partner. "You know what I'm trying to say."

Chast nodded, and Tulliver nodded as well, and after a few nods, both of their chins were nodding in perfect sync.

Matt stood up to leave.

"I was afraid of this," said Tyra. "Matt can't help us out because he's tired. Tired from traveling halfway across the world to see if his ex-wife is still alive. He was stopped by a vampire patrol before he could get to her."

She looked up to see if Matt was engaged and, when it appeared as if he was, she continued.

"I bet if he were to help you guys with a map of the local area, which would be invaluable because Matt grew up around here, you would promise to return the favor by going to his ex-wife's homestead and checking to see if… she was doing all right. Perhaps even leave a message for her…"

"We could do that," Chast said.

"We *would* do exactly that," Tulliver clarified.

"Yes, we would do exactly that," Chast said correcting himself.

"A detailed map of the area around the camp would really come in handy."

Matt took a heavy breath… before sitting back down on the bench.

"What are you getting out of this?" Matt asked Tyra.

"Still doing my job. When I was in the Green Zone working for the State Department, I was known as 'the facilitator.' I was the one who made things happen…"

He turned his attention to the guys. "When are you all making the break?" "It all goes down tomorrow night," said Tulliver, with as much excitement as he could manage while keeping the volume of his voice to a whisper.

"Did you say 'night'?"

"There's a twenty-to-one prisoner-to-guard ratio…"

"… and wide gaps in the compound left unguarded," said Tulliver, interrupting Chast. "Once we cut our way through the fence, the plan is to find a place to hide in the woods until sunrise."

"That's where you come in. Help us find the right place to wait out the pursuit," said Chast, finishing the pitch, "… and we'll be home free."

"Guys, what you're planning is a suicide mission."

Matt's words and his tone came down like a black curtain.

Chast and Tulliver were ready to voice their protest, but Matt continued.

"There's a twenty-to-one ratio at night because who needs guards when the compound is swarming with vampires. The bloodsuckers are capable of seeing a rat's dick swinging from a mile away…"

"We hear you…" interrupted Chast.

"No, you're not hearing me," interrupted Matt right back. "If I sketch a map of the local area, I will make sure to mark with a big black dot the Halcyon Hills mortuary, because that's where all three of you guys are going to wind up if you try to escape at night."

At least Tulliver waited for some silence to pass before he vocalized his disagreement. "We respect what you have to say…"

"Absolutely. Nothing but respect," interrupted Chast.

"… but we have 110 percent confidence in our plan. We really just need your help on the map," said Tulliver.

Matt looked over at Tyra, but she had her head turned away, clearly refusing to make eye contact with him. He dropped his head so that he was looking at his food.

"We're doing this," said Chast. "With or without your help…"

"Okay, I'll draw you guys up a map," said Matt without looking up. "I'll include a few places you can hide when the vampires come looking for you." He finally looked up. "And I'll put in the directions to my ex-wife's house, along with a message."

"That's great!"

"Fantastic. Thanks!"

He stood up, but before he walked away he turned to Tyra.

"None of this means I'm a team player. Hope we're clear on that."

Before she could offer a reply, he walked away.

"Thanks, Tyra, for the hookup," said Chast.

"Yes, dude, we totally owe you," said Tulliver.

"Excuse me…," said Murphy.

Chast and Tulliver turned to look at their third partner.

"Did either of you digest a single word that guy said?" Murphy's face was flushed red and covered in beads of sweat. "He called the plan a 'suicide mission'."

Murphy enunciated the last two words with as much emotion as he could sum up while still whispering. But his dramatic enunciation still fell on deaf ears.

"Jesus, Murph, you're freaking me out," whispered Chast.

"I know. What the fuck?" seconded Tulliver.

Chast took a deep breath, then threw his arm around his former business associate, hoping it would chill him out.

"Listen to me, Amigo, how many times did the three of us hear those exact same words – 'suicide mission' – before we ended up working together at the company's paintball-team tournament?"

"About a thousand times," Tulliver immediately answered in case Murphy was not going to come up with the answer.

"Exactly," said Chast. "And now tell me, Amigo, how did each one of those tournaments turn out…?"

CHAPTER TWELVE

The veteran prisoners in the camp referred to it as the dairy farm. And now the entire prison population of the CCC facility stood in a single-file line waiting to enter into the building.

Standing in line, Matt watched some activity going on at the infirmary building. He saw Dietz walking with two of the camp's guards as they loaded a body bag into a van. After they shut the doors, the van drove past all of the other prisoners standing in line.

"'Meat Wagon' right?" Speaking up was Lee Chong, an Asian-American who was blind. "I can smell the dead body."

"Yeah, Lee, you called it," said Tyra.

"All I can smell is the exhaust from the truck," said Juarez.

"So who's the one getting the ride in the hearse?" asked Chong.

"One of the goons thought he had a shot at the batting title and went too far with a newbie," said Barrett. "He died this morning in the infirmary."

Matt was standing nearby and could hear their conversation. He had a strong feeling about who it was that had died, but hoped he was wrong.

"I think Dietz said his name was 'Bunny'."

None of the prisoners that were talking seemed to recognize the name.

"Where are they taking the body?"

All the prisoners involved in the conversation were shocked to discover the source of the question.

"Who just spoke?" asked Chong

"The shithead I was telling you about... I'm sorry, I meant to say one of the newbies," answered Barrett.

No one stepped up to answer Matt's question, until Tyra finally spoke up.

"We made requests to bury our dead here in camp, but they turned us down. The vampires insist on burying the dead in the woods about two miles from here."

"Does anyone know why?" asked Matt.

"Apparently the bloodsuckers can't stand the smell of rotting cadavers," answered Chong, "even if the body is buried. Can't say I blame them. It's hard for me to put up with the way Juarez smells even when he's downwind from me..."

Juarez pretended to be offended, and shouted, "Yeah, well, you may have to smell me, but I have to look at your ugly face, so that makes us even..."

The main doors to the dairy farm flew open, and a dozen of the goons holding batons filed out and surrounded the line of prisoners.

Spector was the last to emerge. He stood in the doorway, looking out to the line of prisoners like he was the king of the castle addressing his serfs.

"Okay, juice boxes, most of you know the drill, and the rest of you should just follow along so we can all make the entire process run as smooth as possible. That would make me very proud... "

The interior of the building was very similar to a dairy-farming facility. There were hundreds of stalls with complex machinery that looked like it was meant to extract milk from a cow, however, what was being extracted was not milk, but blood.

Matt was part of a single-file line of prisoners, who were led across the building floor and positioned in front of their own stall.

Stepping into his pen, Matt took too long looking at the machinery and felt the tap of a baton to his backside.

"You can daydream all you want once you're wired up," said the goon standing behind him. "Get in there. Now."

The goon shut the door behind him. He looked around and the last thing he discovered was a hook attached to the pen door. Apparently that was where he was supposed to hang his clothes before he wired himself up to be milked.

Spector's voice came over the building's loudspeaker system. "Since we have some new juice boxes joining the party today, I will run through the procedures of your blood donation."

He looked around for Spector, but all Matt saw was a control center on a platform in the middle of the building manned by dozens of black-shirted goons.

"Everyone is to strip, then begin hooking yourself up to the donor machine in your containment area. There are instructional cards posted on the walls above your donor machine. One of my men will come by to make sure you are properly hooked up. C'mon, ladies and gentlemen, let's not make this into anything more than it has to be; the sooner you give two pints, the sooner we can all get out of here…"

Matt stared at the stainless-steel, blood-donation machine. It had six connection pads, each attached to six long, twisty, plastic tubes that eventually flowed together and became a single thick, plastic tube, which then connected to the mouth of a steel container.

The noise in the building helped camouflage the whirling noise coming from the first pad Matt held up for observation. But when he held it closer to his ear, he could hear the almost silent running of the extraction needle moving below the surface of the pad.

He waved his finger directly over the middle of the pad, and almost immediately the tip of his finger was ripped up by a translucent spike whirling in every direction, like a weed whacker, as it tried penetrating the surface of his skin.

The voice of one of the goons advancing toward his stall prompted Matt not to delay the inevitable, and he slapped the first donor pad to his right arm, exactly where a nurse would have stuck an intravenous needle before the takeover.

Matt flinched as the weed-whacking spike tore aside the surface of his skin, drilled toward the nearest vein, which it then penetrated. It wormed at least another inch before resting and embedding itself, and then the process of extracting blood commenced. He turned to see his blood shooting through the clear, plastic tubing toward the steel canister.

The first goal of every system of torture is to strip the victim of their humanity.

After he was completely wired up, and one of the goons had signed off on all his connections to the donor machine, Matt was left completely alone in his pen to contemplate what the vampires had achieved.

They had come up with a form of torture with the assumption that their victim had already been stripped of their humanity.

CHAPTER THIRTEEN

Ian hung from the barracks' ceiling, staring down at Matt as he slept.

Anyone who might have looked up, if they noticed him at all, would only have seen what appeared to be a shadow cast from the moonlight streaming through one of the two barracks' building skylights.

He had shared a room with his little brother until Matt was twelve. Ian would often lie awake and stare at his brother, who always slept like the problems of the world could wait to be dealt with until morning. It was this specific image – content, almost "clueless" about the problems that lay around him – that kept Ian anchored to the bedroom, their house, even though every fiber in his body screamed to escape.

At twelve, their parents agreed to allow Matt to have his own room. It was a huge concession. Ian and his parents all knew that leaving Matt alone in his own room would only make it easier for him to dream about being further away.

As Ian stared at his brother from the ceiling, he couldn't believe the irony of the situation. He had stayed behind at the house because he was afraid of what would happen to Matt if he abandoned him. Now here he was, years later, once again looking over his youngest brother, and his greatest fear was that Matt would abandon him.

***

Winston Gaiman had his eye on a computer screen that spewed out the latest directory notes released by the Vampire Committee. When he finally looked up, he was dismayed to only see Ian standing before him.

"Where is Julian?"

"I don't know, sir," answered Ian.

"Certainly he knew I needed to speak to both of you?"

It had been awhile since Ian had seen Winston looking so exasperated and irritated. The fact that Julian Macy had missed so many previous meetings, and that somehow his latest absence was causing his mentor distress, was troubling to Ian.

"I saw him an hour ago, moving along the perimeter of the camp. I mentioned to him that we would be meeting with you later, but he did not respond in any way."

There was the noise of another directive coming through, and it grabbed Winston's attention. As he stared at the computer screen, a look of concern took over his face.

Ian was sure that if Julian *had* attended the meeting, Winston would not be so open about expressing his emotional reaction to what he was reading.

The CCC commander looked up to Ian and picked up the conversation where he had left it... more than a few minutes ago.

"Are you saying he did not respond to what you said...?'

"No, sir, what I meant to convey was that Julian did not respond to my very presence."

The commander shook his head in dismay.

When Winston was assigned command of what turned out to be CCC197, the first decision he made was to select who would serve as the head of operational control. He could have gone outside his bloodline and chosen someone else. But he stayed loyal to the two he had turned – first Julian, then Ian.

Both of his scions would share the duties of operational control of the facility. Ian would focus on the outreach beyond the perimeter, while Julian would handle all of the issues associated with running the camp.

"It was obvious Julian was not pleased with my decision to divide supervision of the facility, which I anticipated. However, that was months ago. How would continuing to harbor such ill will be a productive course of action?"

"Sir, what would you have me say?"

"I would want you to say something..."

"I don't agree with him... sir."

"Then why aren't you doing something about it...?"

Winston's words shocked Ian, and he did not bother to hide his reaction.

There was another directive coming in from the committee, and Winston turned his attention to his computer screen.

The two had been bonded in blood for years, but Ian had always felt the two were even closer in spirit as well. And yet now that the takeover plan was in full swing, it appeared that the events of the last several months had ruffled Winston's normally calm disposition. Perhaps the frustrations of dealing with the VC had started to wear him down.

Several more minutes passed before Winston looked up from his screen, but Ian did not give his mentor the chance to speak first.

"Julian does not consider my existence worthy of acknowledgment. More than two hundred years separates us in age, and perhaps that's what prevents the two of us from ever achieving a bond that goes beyond the inherited bloodline we share. Sir, with all due respect, what exactly would you have me do?"

"Remind him that you share my bloodline."

He waited for clarification, but when he remained silent, Ian had no choice but to run with what he assumed Winston had implied by his remark.

"Are you suggesting that I remind Julian by spilling his blood, the one thing that binds the three of us...?"

"I suggest you do what is necessary. I believe even without my counsel, Julian will be seeking the same."

Ian was speechless. All he could fathom was that the turmoil of the takeover had somehow driven Winston to suggest such a repulsive course of action.

"I've never told you about the circumstances surrounding my decision to turn Julian?"

Ian shook his head, hoping his continued silence would invite Winston to speak freely about a subject he'd been curious about for as long as he could remember.

"Of course you know Roland Elridge's old adage – 'the living often declare the world has changed, but what remains the same is the changing faces of the living who utter those words'."

"Yes, sir, of course."

The camp commander nodded, stood up, and moved from behind his desk to the window that overlooked the main compound.

"The world has not changed. It has always been the same. But before the takeover, what the living were doing was cruel and horrific, beyond our wildest imagination..."

Winston stopped and chuckled to himself.

"I know. Not much of a statement, because every vampire knows …"

"… those of our kind do not have much of an imagination," said Ian.

He knew his mentor would receive his interruption and completion of the adage as a compliment of his teachings.

"But try to imagine that the world I plucked Julian from was the cruelest I had ever seen... until recent events. At the time I believed an escape from such horrific circumstances would free him so that he could start anew. But my observation of Julian all these years..."

Winston fell silent, as if he was playing back in his head every moment they had spent together.

"… my observation has led me to conclude – those who are turned can't help but reflect the circumstances at the time of their rebirth. The echoes of our past life stay in our heart... even though the heart no longer beats."

He turned to look at Ian.

"My loved one, please understand; the music that has played in your brother's mind has been playing for centuries. It has managed to overwhelm any other notes that he has had the opportunity to hear. Elridge was wise in his words when he said – 'The world changes, the living remains the same, and vampires will'…"

"…'see both the world and the living through eyes forever open'."

The final part of a commonly known phrase, shared for thousands of years amongst their kind, was spoken by the two of them together.

The sound of another VC message coming through on the computer interrupted the silence.

Winston moved quickly to his desk and began reading the communique.

He knew it was not Winston's intention, but after waiting more than ten minutes, Ian decided to accept the circumstances as a silent dismissal.

"Ian…"

He was about to close the door behind him when Winston called out to him.

"Yes, sir…"

"The three of us must talk."

Winston's words were spoken without once turning away from the computer monitor.

"I understand, sir."

CHAPTER FOURTEEN

Ian knew well the species he had originally been born into.

All were "pattern seekers."

It was part of their original genetic code.

His strategy of accumulating more blood donors had been to assign patrols to work a circular sweep within a five-mile radius of the CCC facility. The success of his strategy had been based on his decision to schedule all the sweeps at exactly the same time, lasting for exactly the same amount of time. Every day.

Then he changed the pattern.

Ian would randomly choose a night to assign all the patrols to make their rounds thirty minutes earlier or later. It didn't matter which. Either way, the patrols on that one night always would rope in a new collection of blood donors.

"We've got two donors moving through Sector RR85." The alert came over Ian's walkie-talkie less than a minute after they had begun their second sweep of the night.

He knew the sector very well. It was Halcyon Ridge, a township that once serviced the needs of the Morris canal, which had been in operation for about a century. From the 1820s to the 1920s, the area included an inn, a general store, a church, a watermill, and a blacksmith shop, which serviced the mules that serviced the canal.

Halcyon Ridge was also where Ian had his first job as a busboy at an Italian restaurant.

Heat was radiating from two humans hiding behind the garbage cans in the alleyway of the Rocklin Bar and Grill. It was in that same back alleyway where Ian first kissed Kathy Peterson, who turned out to be his first girlfriend.

His outreach team had yet to come across a potential donor who chose to commit suicide rather than be taken. Though they still followed the VC-recommended acquisition technique implemented months ago in response to all the self-inflicted wounds by potential donors that had occurred during the first weeks of the takeover in the Eastern Hemisphere.

The rest of his team served as the "decoy." They would make their presence known immediately while they encircled the perimeter. While the target donors focused on what seemed like an impending attack, he would suddenly swoop in and apprehend the donors flatfooted.

Oftentimes one of the donors in play would jackrabbit from the hiding space. This was expected and planned for.

Tonight's quarry did not disappoint.

As Ian moved along the roof toward the alleyway, one of the donors bolted across the parking lot.

None of his patrol made a move to stop him until he was out of the view of the other, who still remained hiding.

As Ian silently descended, he could see the other donor was not even looking to see how his friend had fared in his flight from their hiding spot. He was too busy getting loaded on a 1.7 liter bottle of Ketel One Vodka.

Ian waited before announcing his presence. The donor only realized he had company when he went for another swig and discovered Ian was holding the bottle.

"How long had it been since your last drink?" Ian asked.

"Six weeks, three days…"

"And how many hours?"

"Five. Can I have just one more taste before you take me in…?"

He handed him the bottle.

Ian let him drink more than a third of the bottle, then grabbed it from him.

"That's enough. It's been six weeks, three days, and five hours. We don't want you to get sick…"

After helping the man stand, Ian marched him across the parking lot to a member of his team, who would lead him the rest of the way to the transport truck, which would have him to the CCC camp just after daybreak.

He had been leading the outreach program for months, and there was an element of his nightly ventures that continued to repeat itself, to the point that it had stopped surprising him – many of the living he had taken in often greeted him with relief. They had been hiding for so long, and seemed to welcome his gentle touch and guiding hand. Their capture put an end to the running, hiding, and hunger. It also meant that they would no longer have to take care of themselves.

**

He grabbed Matt by his right wrist.

Then he sweated and strained as he pulled him up to the center beam in the barn.

If his little brother had fallen, he would probably have died.

And Ian would have blamed himself.

Even his parents would have blamed him.

Maybe not immediately, but one of them would have said something, even if it was years after Matt's funeral.

"Why weren't you looking after him...?"

All of those thoughts ran through Ian's brain as he stood on the cold ground of the barn, staring up at the rafters.

After he saved his life, not once did Ian think about the stupidity of Matt's action.

His brother had taken a huge risk crossing the longest beam in the barn's ceiling.

What could he possibly have been thinking about?

He heard a noise.

And in a split second, Ian became one of the shadows in the barn.

There he waited until he was satisfied that what he had heard was his own outreach team in the distance sweeping the nearby area.

Ian entered his parents' family room and looked around.

It was smaller than he remembered.

And the low ceiling felt like it was trying to crush him.

Could things have really changed so much since the last time he had walked around as part of the living?

After the takeover, he had no desire to revisit what he had left behind.

It was another life.

Ian stood at his father's horseshoe bar, next to one of the stools.

Not behind the bar itself.

He would never have dreamed of standing on the other side while his father was alive.

He heard the sound of his father's whistle to get his attention.

"This is for your Uncle Teddy."

His father would then slide to him a glass of something he had mixed together that promised to make Uncle Teddy remember what it was like to be… alive.

Bernard Rickard Haynes.

Clara Maria Haynes.

Years ago his father and his mother's full names was what Ian stared at before he read the rest of their obituaries. They had died in an auto accident while travelling north to meet with a real-estate agent to sell their vacation home on one of the Canadian islands.

He read only the first two paragraphs.

Whatever else had been written about his mother and father would be coming from someone else. Maybe even someone who didn't know them at all.

One of the most important rules about being a "shadow" was to embrace the concept that what the living did accomplish was not ultimately important. Any achievement, of any stature, would eventually disappear and become insignificant with the passing of time.

"Those riding the train do not see what those who stand at the station staring at the passing trains see," wrote Lehand Mast.

But Ian could think of nothing that Winston had said or quoted that could stop the pain he felt as he finally got up enough courage to stand behind his father's bar.

As he stood there, Ian looked all around the room, trying to see what his father might have seen.

Then his eyes caught sight of his father's humidor right underneath the bar. It was where he would store his cigars. There was a scotch taped note to the lid that read simply, "Mom & Dad."

Ian recognized the handwriting.

He was forced to look away.

And then he was forced to step away.

Everything about death repulsed his kind.

But Ian forced himself to return back behind the bar.

He took off the lid and saw the ashes of both his father and his mother. He could smell their very essence floating from the box to his nostrils.

The stink of death began to overwhelm him, even as he tried feeling something about the sight of his parents' wedding rings resting atop the ashes.

Ian was about to slam shut the cigar box when he saw something else that stopped him.

It was a dog-eared card that looked like it had been carried around in his father's wallet or his mother's purse for years.

He grabbed the card and dropped the lid back onto the box of ashes.

It was a clipping entitled "The Chimes Before Midnight," and had 12 edicts matching the numbers on a clock.

I
Believe your existence matters in this world.
But never live like you are the center of the universe.

II
Our life on this planet is relatively short.
Some we love will have an even shorter life.

III
Beware of predators amongst us who kill or maim.
Sometimes with no discernible reason.
Someone we trust, even love, may be one of the predators.

Ian stopped reading after the third edict. He dropped the clipping, and fled the house where he had grown up.

He no longer needed any words of comfort from his mentor or any of his kind who had crossed before him.

What he had read only reaffirmed that he had made the right choice a lifetime ago.

His parents would never have understood the fate he had embraced.

CHAPTER FIFTEEN

It was just a little past 3:00 a.m. when the CCC alarms blared through the barracks building.

Seconds later the doors were thrown open and the goons rolled in.

"Okay, juice boxes, assemble immediately in the compound!"

The order was repeated three times through the loudspeakers as the prisoners all tried to respond.

Tyra did not move. She was staring at the ceiling in dread.

A baton tap from one of the goons finally got her to hop out of her bunk and join the rest of the prisoners. As she walked with the others, Tyra was aware of a low-level grumble about being awakened in the middle of the night. But she knew their discontent would be swept into silence once they realized this was not a drill.

Approaching one of the exit doors to the barracks building, Tyra caught sight of someone she did not expect to see – Eric Murphy. Confusion quickly gave over to optimism. Perhaps what she had dreaded was not the cause for the late-night assembly.

"I thought you guys were going out tonight?"

Murphy couldn't look at Tyra as he responded to her question. "Chast and Tulliver did go out tonight, but I changed my mind." He then sped up, so he was not forced to answer any more of her questions.

Other prisoners brushed past her as Tyra stood there, afraid to join the assembly, frightened about what she now felt sure was waiting in the compound.

Matt was about to move past her, but then stopped.

They looked at each other.

All she could see was a face without a trace of guilt.

He had warned them – "Suicide mission."

Her words to him – "I'm a facilitator... The person who makes things happen... "

Before Matt could say a word, Tyra broke away, cutting across the flow of streaming prisoners, to the building's latrines.

She rushed into one of the stalls and threw up into the toilet.

Before she threw up again, she began to cry.

It was the first time Tyra had shed any tears since she had come to the CCC camp.

All of those who had assembled turned as they heard a noise coming from the security building. The door flew open and, after an advanced guard stepped aside, Spector emerged. He was followed closely by Chast and Tulliver, both being dragged by the collar of their prison fatigues by a pair of CCC goons.

As they made their way across the dirt of the compound, each of the captured men tried to regain their own footing, but their efforts to reclaim some dignity before they met their fate fell short.

When the guards released Chast and Tulliver in front of the rest of the prisoners, they both collapsed to the ground – two piles of beaten, battered, and almost lifeless mounds of flesh.

A subsequent noise coming from the black tower turned the heads of the assembled prisoners.

Julian Macy emerged from the cloud of darkness surrounding the base of the tower. However, he was almost halfway across the compound before any of the prisoners could see him.

He was thin, pale, his skin almost completely transparent as beams of moonlight shone down upon the CCC compound.

Julian's appearance was consistent with all the previous sightings of the vampires during the takeover.

But there were also distinct differences.

Unlike some of the bloodsuckers, who could be unsightly and repulsive in the clear moonlight, Julian was eerily beautiful, with jet-black eyebrows, crystal-blue eyes, and chiseled cheekbones that made his appearance hypnotic and alluring.

The way he moved was also of note.

His approach to the assembly of prisoners was as if he controlled all of the airspace around him, as if Julian was walking on air.

Four other vampires emerged from the shadows a few paces behind Julian. None of them had the presence, style, or power of their leader, but all four were moving in lockstep with whatever or however their leader rolled.

This occasion marked the second time Tyra had seen all five. Her first experience came as a result of one her punishments.

While she was waiting in a grey-building stall, Julian came in first, followed by the others. All five of the vampires sported chains around their neck with beautifully carved wooden stakes attached.

Clearly the wardrobe accessory was hung in plain sight for anyone who dared to dream about killing a vampire.

Later, when she recounted the experience to the other prisoners, she referred to Julian's entourage as the "Bat Pack." The moniker stuck, but she regretted the reference over the following months, because it downplayed the fear and respect she not only had for the "Bat Pack," but their leader.

Julian planted himself next to Spector. The head of CCC security wasn't bothering to sell the close proximity of the vampire as an honor.

Since the last time all the prisoners saw him, Spector's intimidating stature had undergone a transformation. Now he stood in front of the assembly with several lines of perspiration running a track meet down his face, along with patches of flop sweat soiling his black uniform, which completely contradicted the dry, cool, early morning temperature.

He took his time before actually addressing the gathering. Julian stared at the prisoners with his crystal-blue eyes as he slowly pulled a pair of black, leather gloves off of his hands.

"Some of you standing before me are recent arrivals. But the rest of you are not new to our system. All of you should have known better."

Julian folded his gloves and put them into his long, dark coat.

"No matter. Tonight all of you will come together in a shared experience that I'm positive will prove to be… life-changing."

Those prisoners who were watching, but blinked at that very moment, would be convinced that Julian had vanished.

Instead, he had moved, like only a vampire can cover ground - without being seen - to be suddenly standing in front of Ron Chast.

The prisoner was barely conscious, his pummeled head falling side to side.

Julian's body blurred for a split second, then somehow… was standing right next to Spector again.

Blood sprayed from two puncture wounds on Chast's neck.

A few away, the Bat Pack waited, like well-trained dogs salivating for their food.

Chast fell face-first into the already sizeable puddle of his own blood, and Julian allowed the sensation of the splash to settle over the other prisoners before he snapped his fingers.

The Bat Pack swarmed Chast like ants attacking an outsider who had fallen to die near the entrance of their colony.

Tulliver's weary eyes had watched his friend's demise, but suddenly his view of the desecration to Chast's body was blocked.

Julian was on his knees, inches from the fugitive prisoner's face.

"There's something you won't be using anymore…"

The vampire stood up, and all the prisoners flinched when they saw Tulliver's still-beating heart in Julian's hand.

The organ stopped beating at exactly the same time that the body it had been snatched from fell to the dirt.

Julian once again addressed the prisoners. "I've been walking amongst you for over two hundred years and this is what I've come to believe – The living end up behaving as if they are truly alive only when facing impending death."

The vampire tossed the heart in his hand onto Tulliver's back.

"Yes, yes, I know… it is a sad conclusion, but it's also an existential reality that all of you must make holy from this point on. If you doubt my word, then just ask yourself: how am I feeling at this very moment?"

The final word had just left his lips when Julian seemingly vanished, only to appear in front of one of the prisoners standing in assembly.

It was Matt. Julian scraped his index finger across Matt's cheek, then swiped what he had gathered across his tongue.

"Ooooh, la, la... AB negative," said Julian with a mischievous grin. "Very rare. If there was a god, you should be thanking him right about now."

Suddenly, Julian was standing in the row directly behind Matt, in front of another prisoner, Warren Hamilton.

The vampire swept his finger across Hamilton's cheek and his tongue shot out from his mouth for the taste test.

"O negative. Not your lucky day..."

Hamilton felt a sting on his neck.

He staggered for a few steps… reached out to one of the other prisoners, then dropped to the ground.

The punctures in Hamilton's skin released a torrent of blood, as if his neck was a fire hydrant in New York City releasing water on a hot summer day.

The prisoners standing nearby attempted to flee, but were curtailed by the goons using their batons to keep them in line. All ended up being completely drenched by the geyser of blood spewing from Hamilton.

Julian was back in front of the assembly, using a silk towel to wipe his hands.

"I hope all of you agree that we're all just players in a drama that goes on night after night. Tonight is dress rehearsal meant to highlight the casting possibilities that have suddenly become available."

The vampire strolled over to the bodies of Chast and Tulliver.

"The parts of the 'rebel prisoners' are now open for recasting. Anyone interested in auditioning for the part?"

Julian scanned the prisoners.

"No takers. I understand."

The vampire moved toward the assembly. His walk was not often seen, so it was amazing to watch how Julian moved across the dirt of the compound like a panther moving confidently around the prey he has already killed.

"Perhaps some of you will consider auditioning for the role of the tragic, innocent victim."

Julian raised the silk handkerchief, now covered in Hamilton's blood. He went through the motions of waiting for an answer.

"Ah, yes, I understand. The part doesn't receive any mention in the program; not exactly a role that an actor can use to build a resume."

He moved back to the front of the assembly.

"Those of us in charge of this production had hoped all of you would be satisfied to play the roles originally assigned to you – as the background talent. And we're still optimistic that the production could go on to great acclaim without ever casting another actor in the roles I've mentioned."

He fell silent as if he was finished. But then he looked up to all the gathered prisoners with a grin that his undead state allowed to take up half of his face.

"Just in case any of you had any silly ambitions of playing the part of 'the star,' let me squash such a notion right now…"

The Bat Pack had long ago finished with Hamilton's corpse, turning it into a dry, empty shell. They were now moving through the assembly like rabid dogs and pawing at the prisoners that had stood nearby. His entourage was licking a face, sucking on fingers, grazing through a scalp of thick hair that had been sprayed with blood.

But they all came to attention when they heard Julian snap his fingers.

A second snapping of his fingers had all of the Bat Pack surrounding Julian, pretending to take pictures of him from imaginary cameras.

After striking a few poses, Julian waved his entourage away.

"If the curtain goes up and we are not all together on the stage, those who tried to leave us will be found, tortured, and killed. And the rest of the company will suffer as well. For every one who is not here, ready for the next performance, twelve of you, chosen randomly, will be tortured and killed as well."

Julian took a deep breath.

"Please understand, this was all very difficult for me. I'm old school. We believe the drama should always remain between the lawyers and the agents, not anywhere near the stage."

The vampire looked around at the prisoners, then turned to Spector. "Get them out of my sight and smell."

The head of security shouted out to the prisoners, "Okay, juice boxes, return to the barracks until our normal morning roll call."

After making the announcement, the head of CCC security turned to apologize for the security lapse.

But Julian was gone.

Spector looked around… and discovered the vampire had retreated into some shadows nearby. There was a disjointed, bony finger waving for the head of CCC security to join him.

Once they were under the umbrella of darkness, Julian spoke aloud his misgivings to the stooge he had appointed to run the camp security.

"If you no longer have the capacity to perform your job, let me know now and we can begin to discuss your severance package."

"Sir, that won't be necessary," Spector said. There was a tremble in his voice that betrayed his fear that they had moved into the darkness because he was going to join the three slaughtered prisoners.

"Then what is the problem?"

"The problem, sir, is that there's only so much I can do to keep the donors in line while staying within the perimeters of your orders not to permanently injure any of them…"

The vampire flashed his crystal-blue eyes, which caused Spector to fall silent and bow his head.

But when Spector didn't hear Julian speak for awhile, he looked up to discover…

The vampire was gone.

One of the goons wasn't happy that Matt continued to stay there and stare at the three dead prisoners. He shoved him with his baton. When he still didn't move, the guard smashed the baton into his gut, which caused Matt to double over and nearly fall to his knees. He was barely able to maintain his balance; it took his feet shuffling in the dirt as if he was learning some new dance step.

When he finally was able to stand straight again, he looked up at the guard, who remained hovering near him, ready to deliver another blow.

It took a baton blast to his gut to make him feel better. The pain shooting through his entire body was what he needed to finally feel whole again.

He was grateful for what the goon had done, and tried to show his appreciation with a smile.

CHAPTER SIXTEEN

As the sun began to rise, Matt was still staring out from one of the barracks' windows. The remains of Hamilton, Tulliver, and Chast were being cleaned up by the goons and stuffed into military body bags.

However, for the last half hour his attention had been divided. Matt had also been watching some activity beyond the fence, where an armored delivery truck was parked beyond the security checkpoint, outside the compound gate. Goons were hauling stainless-steel coolers out to the vehicle and loading them in the back.

In another part of the same building, Barrett was peeping out his own window, making sure the area was completely clear of any goons patrolling nearby.

Satisfied the timing was right, he scrambled across the shower area, where a dozen empty stalls were running water. The noise and the steam, was meant to camouflage the covert gathering taking place in the only shower stall not running water where a group of prisoners had gathered: Tyra, Barrett, Dietz, Juarez, Murphy, Chong, and Grouse.

"Okay, most of the goons are having breakfast," said Barrett. "The others are still focused on cleaning up the mess from last night."

Juarez made it a point of looking over at Murphy for a reaction, but Murphy had his head down, and he was staring at the tile floor.

Tyra stepped into the middle of the group as a way of getting everyone's attention. "I think it's time we... do something."

"Like what?" asked Juarez.

"What we've been talking about for the last several months," answered Tyra. "A plan to escape…"

Everyone in the circle reacted, which got Barrett to raise his hands to quiet everyone down.

"After what we just witnessed?" said Juarez. "No offense, but you either have balls where your brain should be... or no brain at all."

Tyra wasn't sure how to react to Juarez's statement. If she let it go, then maybe no one would respect her enough to listen to what she had to say. But if she tried to make Juarez eat his words, the whole meeting could swing in the wrong direction.

"If either is true," said Dr. Dietz, "you should come to the infirmary later today and let me check into that situation."

The group laughed, and whether he intended it or not, Tyra was grateful the doctor had helped her avoid a confrontation.

"Here's what I see happening," said Tyra. "New prisoners are being brought into the camp every two to three days. It's just a matter of time before the vampires have the luxury of choosing younger, healthier donors for their blood supply. Does anyone want to guess what happens then?"

"We'll all be elevated to Emeritus status...," answered Chong.

Dietz was the only person who laughed at the remark.

"This is a tough crowd," Chong mumbled to himself.

"Ty, you heard Macy: any attempt to get out of here will result in the death of twelve prisoners for any of us who tries to escape," said Barrett.

"Believe me, I heard every word coming from that bloodsucking leech," Tyra replied. "Which means we only have one option if we're going to guarantee the safety of all the prisoners in the camp."

She paused to make sure everyone in the shower stall was paying attention. Even Murphy was now looking up at her.

"We need to come up with an escape plan that will set free *all* of the camp prisoners."

Her idea was initially greeted with stunned silence.

Then Juarez turned to Dietz. "Doc, I need to see you tomorrow; there's something wrong with my hearing. I think I just heard Ty say something about the entire camp is going to escape!"

The group encircling her turned away. Most didn't want to laugh right in her face. But certainly Tyra saw that everyone was snickering or shaking their heads to her proposal.

It was once again Barrett who tried to speak rationally to her.

"Ty, you realize, with the newest arrivals, we're now up to 166 prisoners."

"I know the body count. I hear it twice, every day."

"So, you're serious?"

Before she could respond to Juarez, there was the noise of approaching footsteps. The sound immediately silenced the group.

A figure stepped from the steam into view. It was Matt.

"What is this, like a strategy session?"

Barrett stepped in front of Matt.

"Yeah, something like that."

"That's what I thought."

Matt leaned out to one side so he could see Tyra.

"I'd love to get in on this meeting. Especially if what you're talking about is another escape attempt."

She tapped Barrett on the shoulder to stand aside.

"Matt, I didn't extend an invitation because you made it perfectly clear you weren't interested in being part of… the team."

"Yeah, fair enough…"

He looked around at all the faces staring at him – one of the guys was a psycho and his presence at the meeting spoke volumes about how desperate the situation had become; one guy had lied to him the first day he arrived at the camp and he still wasn't sure if all he had been doing was lying to everyone else so he could stay alive; two of the guys, both in his face at that very moment, were doing their best to pretend they were still in high school; another guy standing in the circle he had seen before, but because he couldn't see him back, he didn't feel the need to even learn his name; the last guy was someone he was sure he had met since he arrived in camp, but somehow his personality wasn't distinct enough to show up on his radar.

And then there was the ringleader.

Matt was sure she had begun life as the child of a father who had originally picked out the name, "Ty," then was forced to switch to "Tyra" when he saw his newborn didn't have a dick.

"… But that was then," said Matt, "this is now."

"Yeah, so how is 'then' and 'now' so different?" asked Juarez, practically spitting the question in Matt's face.

"Before I answer, I just want to make sure Tyra has kept you all up to date on my recent effort." He looked over at her, "You did tell everyone that I drew up a map of the local area. As requested. So even though I might not have been wearing a jersey, there can be no doubt I was committed to playing for the team."

Tyra nodded her head and waved him forward. "He's totally right. I'm glad to see you joining us, Matt. Hey, guys get out of his way…"

Slowly Barrett and Juarez stood aside and allowed Matt to join Tyra in the middle of the circle.

"This is nice," Matt said. "Like the round table… with a lot of steam."

"More like a 'circle jerk'," said Juarez.

Standing next to her, Matt could practically hear the adrenaline that Juarez's words caused to start pumping through Tyra's body.

"Ty here just proposed we sign onboard to an escape plan that frees all the prisoners," said Barrett

Matt looked at her, then hung his head sheepishly.

"Well, now I'm afraid some of you will suspect my appearance was somehow… prearranged."

"What are you talking about?" Tyra said looking at Matt with an incredulous face. "Are you saying you have an escape plan that gets all of us out of here?"

He nodded. "Yeah, I do."

But before he could say another word, Barrett stepped into the middle to the address the others.

"This guy has uttered two syllables since he got here, 'fuck' and 'you.' Now suddenly he wants us to follow his lead."

"I agree with Cliff," Juarez immediately chimed in. "This guy is out for himself. You can see it in his eyes."

"Look, when I first got here," said Matt, "I didn't know who I could trust."

Grouse blurted out, "You still don't. I know a loner when I see one and this guy is completely out for himself."

"I can't believe I'm saying this," said Juarez, "but for once I actually agree with Grouse."

"Fine. I hear you," interrupted Tyra, quickly stepping in before the negativity spread like a cancer through the entire circle. "But tell me this – what's the harm in at least hearing what he has to say?"

No one had an answer. At least, no one standing in the shower stall disagreed strongly enough to speak up.

"Go ahead, let's hear your plan," said Tyra, before stepping back and yielding the center of the circle to Matt.

"Well, as I said before, I happen to agree with Tyra. If we're going to spring a few, we might as well get everyone out of here," said Matt. "The reason I feel that way is because, frankly, getting out of this camp is relatively easy…"

"Chast and Tulliver might raise an objection if either of them was alive," said Barrett.

Matt resisted the urge to look over at Murphy, instead quickly responding to Barrett's objection.

"Actually, you're wrong. Their deaths confirm what I just said. You see, Chast and Tulliver weren't caught on this side of the fence. They were eventually tracked down on the outside."

Matt turned to Tyra and said, "Which is exactly what I warned them would be the problem, right?"

Tyra nodded, and her response was sincere enough to convince the others in the circle to hear more. But Matt also saw the doubt even in her eyes – she was waiting to hear his plan.

"See, the real strategy to escaping from this shithole is what happens after we're on the outside. How do we defend ourselves? What weapons do we use? Where do we go when the vampires start looking for us? Will we be in the right place to fight back? I actually have the answers to all those questions…"

He looked around, trying to gauge how many in the group were listening and who had already tuned him out.

"Sorry about that! I fell asleep right in the middle of the bedtime story," said Juarez. "Hopefully I didn't miss my favorite part about the really tall castle just yonder and how the unicorn kills all the bad vampires…?"

Matt made sure to laugh along with the other prisoners.

Then when he had the floor again, he responded, "You're right, Juarez. If anything I propose sounds like a fairy tale, then we all die… including me."

There was silence, but everyone was listening to whatever Matt had to say next.

"My plan has several steps, but the key to its success is that it involves… two escapes."

Immediately his words triggered a reaction from the group, but Barrett stomped his foot on the shower tile. "All of you keep it down! Besides, I want to hear what he has to say!"

Matt wasn't sure why Barrett took it upon himself to give him a fair hearing, but ran with the opportunity to continue.

"As I said, 'two escapes.' The first one will allow for a trip to a nearby town, to gather a ton of weapons and supplies, which will then be stashed in some key areas, including a strategic stronghold where we'll all make our stand against the vampires."

"What do you have in mind as a 'strategic stronghold'," asked Tyra.

Matt wasn't put off by her question. She could have suspected that the place he had in mind was the same place to which he had directed Tulliver and Chast – his ex-wife's house – which could have been the very place where they were eventually caught.

"My family's old farm," answered Matt. "There's many advantages to going there, including the farm is at the top of a hill. You don't have to be a West Point graduate to know the high ground is always the best place to defend."

"And who exactly goes out during this 'first escape'?"

The question came from Barrett, and Matt noticed that his words had a cynical undertow.

"Because of some necessary requirements for the operation to be successful, my plan only allows for one person to make the escape…"

His answer was buried in a groan of objections from the circle of prisoners. They all knew who Matt would propose to be the one prisoner making the first escape.

Tyra stepped forward with a raised hand that finally quieted the surrounding men. She then asked, "Matt, what's your plan, and why does it only allow for one person to escape?"

He looked around, unsure if he should continue. The more details he shared, the less likely the plan would end up including him. But he realized he had no choice.

"I've noticed the bloodmobile makes two daily trips to the camp – once in the mornings to deliver empty bottles; and then again about ten hours later, before sunset, to pick up the most recent supply of canisters filled with blood."

Tyra shook her head, ashamed that she had totally missed what Matt had noticed after just being here for a few days.

"But since the truck never goes past the first security checkpoint, the bloodmobile would have to be used as the escape back into the camp at the end of the day, hopefully before the second roll call... before any of the goons actually realize that the escaping prisoner had been gone at all."

"I'm sorry," interrupted Chong. "Call me slow, but you just described the way back into the camp. Did I miss the part of the plan about how someone is going to get out?"

"As I said, the bloodmobile never actually drives into the compound," said Matt. "So the way out has to come from a vehicle which enters the main compound so we have the opportunity to hitch a ride out. The only vehicle I've seen that meets those needs is... the cadaver van."

Around the circle, almost everyone reacted with a sense of recognition. They all realized that Matt was right; the cadaver van was the only vehicle allowed into the main compound to pick up any dead bodies, then it would leave the camp to dispose of the corpses.

"My plan puts me in a body bag in the cadaver van, riding out of the compound, out of the camp, then at the perfect time jumping out to begin getting the resources we'll need for the second, bigger escape involving all of the prisoners. And then at the end of the day I hitch a ride on the bloodmobile, getting back to the camp before any of the goons even know that I've been gone."

He looked around and saw a lot of positive reaction to his plan. But Matt also saw a few faces that didn't look so convinced.

One of the naysayers was Barrett, and he was the first to speak. "Look, I admit; what you're pitching is a real plan. But c'mon, how stupid do you think we are? We help you get out of here on the cadaver van; we're supposed to be standing in the main compound with our dicks in our hands, waiting for you to come back…?"

Matt didn't hesitate with a response. "Yeah, that's right. All except for the dicks in your hands part."

"We help this guy escape," said Grouse, "we won't even get a postcard. And then we'll be the ones doing the payback to the vampires."

Juarez chimed in as well. "I hate to agree with Grouse twice in an hour, but I totally am seeing things his way…"

The gathering of prisoners all started to grunt with agreement, until Tyra joined Matt back in the middle of the circle.

"What if I and someone else rolled with you during the first escape?"

There was no need for Matt to look around to verify that it was either he went along with Tyra's suggestion, or there was no chance his plan would get any support.

"As long as you… all of you, are willing to do what it takes to make sure we've got… three body bags."

She knew what that meant if Matt was being sincere and not just trying to scare her off. "What do you think everybody? What if Juarez and I go with Matt for the first escape? Would everyone be cool with that?"

All around the circle there seemed to be a general positive reaction to Tyra's suggestion. Until Murphy spoke up.

"This guy is gonna get us killed."

Murphy looked around the stall.

"I can't believe I'm the only one feeling this way."

Barrett took a few steps toward Murphy, which only caused the objecting prisoner to take a few steps back in response.

"I hear you. Believe me I do. From day one I have not been a fan of this mercenary jackal, but if he's willing to go with Ty and Juarez..."

"No, you're not hearing me! Listen to me, none of you should trust this guy," said Murphy. "Look at him. Stop looking at me and look at him... don't you see what I see? He's on a suicide mission, and he's trying to grab as many people to join him before he crash-and-burns."

"As long as we're talking about crashing and burning, what the hell happened with you and your Wall Street buddies, Chast and Tulliver?" asked Juarez.

Murphy did not hesitate with his answer, though his explanation sounded a bit rehearsed.

"There was a plan. It ended up being a bad plan. And they died. What I want to know is why hasn't anyone come up to me and congratulated me about making the right call?"

Barrett looked around, before being the first to respond.

"Maybe because congratulating you would be like exchanging high fives at the airport after you missed a flight that crash-landed."

"Or worse," said Chong. "I heard the plan needed three men to fly the plane, but someone who was supposed to be in the cockpit grabbed a parachute and bailed."

Murphy's face turned beet red. He slowly started to move backwards, even though no one was moving toward him.

"There's a reason I'm still alive," he mumbled to the group.

"Yeah, for sure," said Juarez. "Hey, where are you going? Stick around. We'll kick around some more reasons and then you can pick the one you want us all to believe."

Several of the prisoners smiled.

"Fuck you. Fuck all of you. Believe what you want."

Murphy then pointed at Matt. "There's no way some hotshot is going to put my name on some lottery ticket."

Tyra raised her hands and started to approach the now completely unhinged prisoner. "Where are you going, Murphy? You need to calm down…"

"Don't even try to tell me what I need to do…," he said, each word getting louder than the last, but then he backed right into a shower-stall wall and the impact scared him into falling silent.

"He's right. Let him go."

All the prisoners turned to verify the words were really coming from… Matt.

"No matter how good my plan is, it's a huge risk," said Matt staring at Murphy. Then he turned to look, one by one at all the other prisoners. "Do me a favor, each one of you here – forget I even said anything."

Murphy didn't wait for any of the prisoners' reaction to Matt's request. Once the spotlight was no longer on him, he scrambled out of the shower stall and disappeared into the surrounding clouds of steam.

Tyra sidled up next to Matt with an incredulous look on her face.

"Just like that… you're punking out?

"No, I'm still in." Matt then turned to look at Tyra… and the rest of the group of prisoners. "And hopefully all of you are still in as well. It's Murphy who is out. Now we have to wait and see what that might mean to our plans…"

CHAPTER SEVENTEEN

Murphy was standing at the end of the second row during the second head count.

All Matt and Tyra could see from the fifth row was the balding back of Murphy's head. Nonetheless, Matt was convinced the former Wall Street analyst had something on his mind. Murphy had spent the entire roll call looking all around the compound as if he were the star of a grade-school play and was trying to locate his parents in the audience.

"166 men present and accounted for, sir."

"Dismiss them," the security supervisor told Williams.

"Okay, you're all dismissed until the next head count."

The prisoners broke formation.

Matt and Tyra turned as if they were talking to each other, but both continued to keep an eye on Murphy, who stayed planted in his spot while all the other prisoners around him scattered in different directions.

"There's Spector," said Tyra.

Matt looked over. On the side of the compound, near the security-staff mess hall, the head of camp security was walking with another one of his goons.

"Perfect. Now we'll get to see if I'm right… or just paranoid.

But then when both of them turned back…

Murphy was gone.

He was smoking a cigarette in the alley between the security-staff barracks and mess hall. Standing there, waiting for Spector to show up, Murphy couldn't resist and opened up one of the three portable BBQs the goons used to cook on the weekends.

The inside of the grill smelled of cooked, red meat. He also caught the whiff of salmon.Murphy closed the BBQ lid the moment he saw a large figure appear at the mouth of the alleyway.

He stamped out his cigarette and rehearsed the first few lines he wanted to use to kick off his tip about a "rebel" being amongst the prisoners. Murphy knew enough about Spector that if his first few words didn't come out right, the head of security might ignore everything else he had to say and dismiss him.

Suddenly, he felt a sharp jab in the small of his back, causing him to grimace and let out a small yelp.

He wheeled around to discover a football at his feet.

"How you doing, Murph…?"

Barrett came running up to him, clearly the one who had thrown the football.

"What are you doing here?" Murphy growled.

"A few of us are getting together for a game. I came to see if you wanted to play."

Before Murphy could respond, a gravelly voice echoed between the two buildings. "What the fuck are you two doing in this area?"

"Oh, shit," said Barrett under his breath, but loud enough for Murphy to hear, "looks like we might be in trouble."

Spector pushed aside one of the potted plants next to a bamboo cocktail bar as he barked at both of the prisoners.

"I hope you two have an believable explanation for why you're in a totally restricted area."

"Actually, sir…," Murphy began.

"We lost our football," Barrett interrupted. He reached down and picked up the pigskin on the ground next to Murphy. "Sorry, but it's the only football we have."

Spector swept his hand across a wooden rack attached to the BBQ, sending all the stainless-steel tools flying.

"You both better get the hell out of here before I make you eat that football!""Absolutely," answered Barrett.

But Murphy protested. "But, sir, if you would just hear me out…"

Spector punched him in the chest.

Murphy collapsed to the ground, gasping for air.

The head of security turned to Barrett. "You better get him out of here this instant or you both will be donating an extra pint today."

"Yes, sir," said Barrett. He grabbed Murphy by the back of his fatigues and dragged him away.

The two emerged into the main compound with Barrett still dragging Murphy across the ground.

Murphy got a hold of his breath, dug his heels into the dirt, and after Barrett released him, awkwardly stood on his own.

"Wow, that was a close one," said Barrett. He tossed Murphy the football.

Murphy initially fumbled the toss, but when he finally got ahold of the football, the prisoner threw it angrily across the compound.

Barrett watched Murphy storm off.

He turned to Matt and Tyra, standing nearby, and flashed an upside-down V with his index and middle fingers. It was the sign that they had all agreed on if someone saw Murphy trying to tell Spector about their meeting.

"I can't believe this is happening," said Tyra.

Matt didn't say a word as he watched Murphy move slowly across the compound.

After his silence became unbearable, Tyra asked, "What are we going to do?"

"It's my fault. I'll take care of this problem."

"Are you saying what I think you're saying?"

All he could do was nod.

"First of all, it's not your fault. Second – there's another option."

He shook his head. "I wish there was. Believe me I've already thought about it. There is no other option."

Her eyes, like Matt's, were watching Murphy walking across the compound, headed to the barracks building.

"I've also thought about it, Matt. What I'm trying to say is that it doesn't have to be you."

When Tyra approached Lincoln Grouse in the mess hall, he was mentally in the middle of planning the death of another prisoner.

"Hey, Lincoln, how is it going?"

Grouse was so startled to hear her voice, and then to see her sitting so close to him, he dropped his fork onto the floor. He bent over to pick up his utensil, but when he came back up he couldn't look at her, nor could he even move.

"What you doing?"

"Relax. I need to talk to you."

Grouse tried his best to start eating, as if Tyra's presence in his space wasn't freaking him out.

"Talk to me about what?"

"Killing someone."

The scowl that Grouse had been wearing since – well, since he had become a prisoner – disappeared.

"Murphy."

She looked away, almost embarrassed by how obvious what they were contemplating was… to a killer.

"Taking Murphy out makes a lot of sense. You should be proud. It's the smartest thing I've heard you say since you've been here."

Tyra used her plastic fork to poke and push at the food on her tray.

"Glad you approve, Lincoln. So I take it that you can make this happen?"

"Pretend you just emerged from a time machine and now you're walking around. The first thing you'll notice is that Murphy is dead."

She kept poking at her food, afraid to look up and see the enthusiasm that was undoubtedly lighting up Grouse's face.

"Wait a second. I need to know something," said Grouse. "Is this coming from you? Or my bunkmate?"

Tyra looked over to Matt, sitting just a few tables away. He had been uneasy about Tyra approaching Grouse, and was watching to see what happened.

"It's coming from both of us."

"Really? So you're saying he requested my services?"

"Yeah. That's right."

Grouse turned to Matt and gave him a nod.

"It's not just us. Everyone at the meeting today is down for this."

"Well, you're all making me feel bad for all the shit I've been whispering behind your backs."

He hoped she would laugh, because he intended it as a joke. But she didn't even crack a smile.

"It needs to happen tonight. After we donate, everyone will head back to the barracks for a shower. Murphy is always one of the last to take his shower. Barrett, Juarez, and I will corral the other prisoners when the time is right. We'll make sure you have the entire area to yourself."

"Beautiful."

He started to get up.

"Grouse…"

He drew a heavy breath and sat back down.

"There's one more, very important detail…"

The noise of a dropped tray by one of the prisoners working behind the food service counter caught everyone's attention in the mess hall… including Grouse. His face quickly settled into a fugue state, one that had a scowl attached to it.

"Grouse? Grouse…?"

The scowl on his face was still there when he looked over at her.

"You have a problem with someone serving the food? Who? Hoffman?"

"What's it to you?" His voice was louder than a whisper and a few of the other prisoners looked over.

She moved closer to him before responding. "I'm asking for you to do something... something really important. But it looks like you can't even keep your priorities straight. That's what it is to me."

Grouse wanted to explode at her words, but he managed to control himself. What Tyra was requesting was just too good for him to pass up. He picked up the rock-hard roll on his plate and stuffed it in his mouth before he could scream himself out of a job.

"What's your problem with Hoffman?"

Once he managed to swallow some of the sourdough in his mouth, he answered her. "That son of a bitch tried to poison me."

"You can't be serious?"

"I was in line for breakfast a week ago, and when it came to my turn, Hoffman suddenly decided to switch serving trays. He dished out my grub from this other steel container, then he closes the tray and goes back to serving the next guy in line from the other tray."

"Maybe he was giving you the kosher meal," said Tyra.

"I'm not a fucking Jew."

"I was kidding," said Tyra.

"So you think this is funny?"

She stood up.

"No, but listening to you makes me realize that our idea was a huge mistake."

Tyra walked away from the table, and across the mess hall. Every step she took, she expected Grouse to stop her. But when she arrived at the garbage bins, dumped her meal into the trash, then exited the mess hall, the psycho prisoner had not budged from his spot on the bench.

Tyra was almost halfway across the compound when she heard Grouse's voice.

"Wait up…"

He approached her with his head down.

"Look, what I said was true. Hoffman is trying to kill me…"

"What… I can't hear you…"

Grouse lifted his head and locked eyes with her for a split second, before looking back down.

"I can put my beef with Hoffman in the freezer if it will make you happy."

"Lincoln, none of this makes me happy. We're all just interested in getting the hell out of here. Now are you a part of that, or what?"

He nodded.

"We're going to need you to strangle him."

It was a small man that made the humiliating walk across the compound. But now Tyra's words allowed him to stand tall again, and meet her eyes with a face flushed with excitement.

"Did you say 'strangled'?"

"Yes. The way he dies needs to match the scenario we're planning for the first escape."

"That will not be a problem. I have a soap-on-a-rope underneath my bunk. My kid gave it to me for Father's Day five years ago. I've been waiting for the right time to use it."

"That's great…"

He started to walk away, but then turned around.

"Don't you want to wish me luck?"

There were times in the Green Zone when some of the new arrivals would be frightened about some rocket fire or an explosion.

The other state-department personnel always elected Tyra to be the one to offer a warm hug and some comforting words. She usually said something like, "It's going to be all right…," or…, "this is going to be a piece of cake."

Her last resort was to say, "Look at me; I'm still standing, right?"

Tyra's effort usually settled the newbie down.

Now, standing in the middle of the compound, a warm hug was out of the question.

And any words of comfort or wishes of good luck would be redundant.

What Tyra had asked Grouse to do was like asking a fish to jump into the ocean and… swim.

But still, all she could think about was being free.

"Yeah, for sure, Lincoln. All of us wish you… good luck."

Then Tyra looked around for a place to sit down, feeling completely unsteady on her feet.

CHAPTER EIGHTEEN

The prisoners had begun to line up outside the white building for their blood donation.

Matt was standing with Barrett and Chong in the middle of the line. All three were nervous, because there was no sign of Murphy. Juarez had been the last one keeping an eye on the traitor, but he wasn't in line either.

Tyra eventually emerged from another part of the compound, and took a place in line next to Matt.

"How are you feeling?" he asked her.

"How should one feel after negotiating their first hit for hire?"

After her answer, Tyra caught herself, making sure she didn't look like she was going through some kind of meltdown. The last thing she wanted to do was hand Matt an excuse to exclude her from the first escape.

"Look, I just want to tell you how much I appreciate what you did. I mean, I already have enough shit that I'm trying to square away."

Tyra felt uncomfortable listening to Matt trying to express himself emotionally – the long pauses between just a few words; the way he was digging the right heel of his boot into the dirt; and the way he avoided eye contact with her.

But she held her tongue until he was finished.

"I heard what you said... and I appreciate it. But, here's the thing... Matt, look at me..."

Matt froze, then cast his eyes in her direction.

"I know it's probably been mostly guys you've been running around with for... probably forever," said Tyra. "I'm not a guy, but there's some advantages that come along with that fact... advantages perhaps you might be overlooking. One of them is that you can... talk to me... about anything."

Matt looked away.

Tyra saw his reaction... then endured his silence... before switching to plan "B."

"Look, I probably should have said something sooner. Now I feel bad, because part of the deal I made with Grouse was for you to make his bed for the next six months."

Matt looked up at her and chuckled.

"Where is the motherfucker?"

Barrett's words not only broke the eye contact between her and Matt, it was the first time Tyra realized that Murphy wasn't standing in line with them.

"He's not here? "

"No sign of him, and we're due to go into the dairy farm any second," said Barrett.

They all scanned the compound.

The silence was broken up by Chong, the blind prisoner.

"Want me to go look for him?"

The group broke out in nervous laughter.

Tyra then caught sight of Juarez emerging from the alley near the prisoners' mess hall.

But he was alone.

"I was following him all around the compound for the entire day and at one point, I could just tell he knew what I was doing," said Juarez as he joined the others in line. "So I handed the surveillance off to Tiello. That was about forty minutes ago."

"Tiello" was Vittorio Salatiello, a young and muscular Italian who had been visiting family in the States when the takeover occurred. Hearing what Juarez had done made Tyra feel better about the situation. She was confident Tiello would be able to handle Murphy if he got out of line.

The doors opened to the dairy farm. Goons rolled out from the main entrance and began to establish their positions up and down the line of prisoners.

"Okay, juice boxes, let's start moving into the building..."

The line surged forward, but Matt, Tyra, and the others stood their ground, waiting for a sighting of either Tiello or Murphy.

"What are you juice boxes waiting for? A private invitation!"

One of the goons was in their faces about the gap in the line.

They all acted as if the guard wasn't speaking to them.

"Start moving or all of you will be heading to the infirmary!"

When he still couldn't get their attention, the goon shoved Juarez.

"There's Tiello," whispered Tyra.

The Italian was entering from the north side, nearest the black tower.

Alone.

But then Murphy appeared, just a few feet behind him.

Tiello knew enough not to approach Juarez or Tyra, instead grabbing a place at the back of the line.

Right in front of Murphy.

When he got a chance, the Italian threw out his chin in their direction. Everything was all right.

The goon slapped his baton hard against Barrett's wide back. He and the goon stared at each other until Barrett shouted out, "C'mon, boys and girls, it's time to give back to the community. Two pints is all they ask…"

When Matt stepped up to be examined by Dietz, he acted like he was dizzy.

"You don't look good?" said Dietz.

"Exactly. Now pretend like you need to examine me for a few more minutes," said Matt, as he looked at the line behind him.

The camp doctor did as he was told, eventually motioning to one of the goons to divert the other prisoners standing in his line.

Matt started to cough.

"Okay, first you pretended to be dizzy, now you're coughing," said Dietz. "Please settle on something so it doesn't look like you're making it up as you go along…"

Matt started blinking his eyes uncontrollably.

"There must be something wrong with your ears. Clearly you're having difficulty hearing a word I'm saying to you," said Dietz.

He turned, blinking his eyes, and looked in all the lines for Murphy, but didn't see him. "Where the fuck is he?" said Matt under his breath.

"Murphy?"

"Yeah…"

In between checking Matt's blood pressure and writing down the figures, Dietz continued to check the lines of prisoners.

"I'm sorry to hear you're feeling ill," said Dietz, as he shone the light into Matt's eyes. "I wish I could be more help…"

He then clicked off the penlight and motioned to one of the goons.

"He's good to go…"

Matt's eyes widened with surprise, which Dietz saw even though he was no longer shining a light toward them.

"Murphy just entered the building," the doctor said under his breath. Then in a louder voice he said to Matt, "Look, your eyes will be fine. Just stop whacking off so much…"

Matt entered his donation stall and began disrobing.

"Are you there Ty?"

"Yeah, right in the next stall," she answered.

"Any sign of him?"

"No, not yet."

Two of the goons entered his stall and looked to make sure Matt had plugged himself into the blood-donation machine.

"Mind if I do the honors?"

"Yeah, go ahead," said Matt. "Glad I could bring some sunshine to your day."

The goon flipped the switch on the machine and exited the stall.

Matt grimaced at the initial sting of the needles plunging into his skin.

"There he is…"

Her words got him to look up, but he couldn't see above the stall door.

Matt carefully stood upright, knowing that if he pulled any of the blood plugs from his body it would send a signal to the main control room and it would trigger a response from the goon squad.

He finally saw Murphy in a stall directly across the way from Matt and Tyra. It was actually on the other side of the dairy-farm building, with about fifty feet dividing the two areas of blood-donation stalls. Smack in the middle of the building was the CCC security office, a glass-encased edifice two stories above all the donation stalls.

"Do you see him?"

"Yeah, I see him."

"And…"

"And we have a problem."

Murphy was not wired up to give blood. Instead he was talking to a goon. When the guard left Murphy's donation stall, he was making a beeline to the main security room.

"Any ideas?"

"Where's Grouse?"

"He's not yet in the building and it will be too late when he gets here."

Matt looked around. He tried to think of something… but nothing was coming to him. It probably didn't help that his blood was rushing from his body so fast the red tubes were starting to blur.

"We can't wait for tonight," Tyra said, her voice just above the hum of the blood-donation machines.

He narrowed his eyes to see that the goon who had been talking to Murphy was headed upstairs to the building's security room.

"We got to do it now. I'm going to disconnect from the donor machine."

"Matt, you won't get twenty feet from your stall before the goons are all over you."

"You're right. That's why you need to get Juarez or Barrett to take care of Murphy. I'll create the diversion."

"Matt... be careful..."

He didn't hear her. Matt was already removing the pads from his body... while he began screaming at the top of his lungs.

CHAPTER NINETEEN

Matt's screams were finally drowned out by the building's alarms.

Tyra didn't think it was possible, but the reverb from the alarm was causing her more pain than the donor plugs siphoning blood from her body.

She waited until the CCC guards moved past her stall before she began ripping off the machine's pads from her skin.

And through it all she kept a watchful eye on Murphy across the way in his stall.

Bang… bang… bang… The goons were trying to gain entry to Matt's stall, but he had used the donation machine's plastic tubing to tie shut the door.

When one of the guards finally kicked open the door to Matt's stall, they saw it was empty. They looked up and saw Matt standing on top of the stall's back wall. He had used the contents of his own donor tube to cover every inch of his skin with blood. As he stood there laughing at the goons, Matt looked like a devilish fiend.

As the guards rushed into the stall toward him, Matt simply leaped over to the next stall wall. He then began running on the narrow beam that divided the different stalls.

Tyra emerged from her pen and grabbed some quick glances up and down the strip that divided the north and south maze of stalls.

There was about one-hundred-twenty-five feet of concrete between where she stood and where Murphy was cowering in his stall.

Juarez and Barrett burst out of their stalls and moved to Tyra.

"Remember, he has to be strangled, and then his body needs to go back to the barracks..."

The two prisoners nodded in unison, then looked at each other.

"Cover me..."

"No, you cover me..."

All three started to make their move, but two prisoners suddenly sprinted past them... followed by four goons waving their batons.

She looked around her. The building had quickly descended into anarchy.

The alarms continued to blare as Matt raced atop one of the main stall walls. There were two different places in the maze of stalls with wide gaps. Both areas had goons waiting for the opportunity to grab their quarry.

But both times Matt leaped across, soaring above the goons swinging their batons in the air.

He turned in the direction from which he had come to see if he could assess the progress of Tyra and the boys, but Matt couldn't make out anything in the chaos.

Tyra, Juarez, and Barrett were weaving their way through the wave of rioting prisoners and the swarm of goons chasing after them. Pockets of fighting turned their efforts to traverse the strip into a virtual crawl.

Through it all, Tyra kept her eye glued to Murphy.

Suddenly, Juarez was hammered across the head by a passing goon. He staggered, but managed to stay on his feet… until the goon followed with a blow to Juarez's leg that dropped him to the ground. As the same goon was pulling back for a third swing, Barrett leaped into the air and tackled him.

Tyra watched Barrett and the goon wrestle across the concrete strip while Juarez lay just a few feet away writhing in pain.

But rather than stopping to help… she kept moving toward Murphy's stall.

A pair of athletic CCC goons were running parallel with Matt as he sprinted along another part of the stall maze.

It was almost as if the three were competing in the Post-Apocalyptic Olympics.

The guards both saw that Matt was heading toward a dead end and were hoping he wouldn't realize it until it was too late.

But then, just as Matt approached the east wall of the building, and there was no other place to run… he disappeared.

The two CCC guards stood outside the stall getting their breath back before they began slamming their bodies against the door. On the third try they burst through... only to have Matt spray both of them with blood from a donor machine still hooked up to probably the only prisoner who had remained hooked up to the juicer throughout the chaos.

Once they were drenched in blood, Matt punched and kicked the blinded guards until they both fell unconscious to the concrete. He then grabbed one of the riot batons and took off running.

The sound of the blaring alarm, and the sight of the total chaos all around him, had chased Murphy to the back of his stall, where he cowered near the blood-donor machine.

He held his breath as the door to his stall suddenly swung open, then immediately relaxed when he saw it was just a woman... Tyra.

Murphy quickly stood up.

"Jesus, what the hell is going on out there?"

She closed the stall door behind her before answering.

"It's Haynes. He was right in the middle of getting milked when he just went batshit."

Murphy started toward her. "What did I tell you about him?! Didn't I say he was going to get us all killed?!!"

"Murphy, you were so right. I should have listened to you..."

She then stepped out of his way as he moved to look over the stall door.

"You're damn right I was right..."

Matt raced around a corner and skidded to a halt when a he saw an approaching guard. He turned to go back the way he came, but there were two more CCC goons. Changing courses again, Matt rushed toward the single guard coming at him. He ducked underneath the goon's first swing, then planted a baton jab to the goon's stomach that doubled him over.

When the goon fell to his knees, Matt was able to see the exit to the dairy building was just a short distance away. He crowned the goon with the butt of his stick and took off running.

Murphy was standing at the door of his stall when he heard some of the prisoners cheering.

"Can you believe this shit? I think they're actually cheering this lunatic on…"

He started to turn around to see if Tyra was watching when one of the plastic tubes from his juicer looped over his head, dropped around his throat, then yanked him off his feet.

The two both slammed hard to the concrete floor.

The impact, and the confusion about what was happening, caused Murphy to delay in fighting back.

But Tyra knew exactly where she was headed.

She quickly dragged his squirming body across the concrete until she was able to plant her feet against the raised cement slab housing the blood-donation machine.

Then she wiggled sideways, until her back was braced against the stall wall.

This was the exact position Tyra held onto as she gained more and more strength, while Murphy slowly lost all of his.

The stall door suddenly flew open.

Barrett and a bloody Juarez rushed in to the stall.

They saw Tyra and Murphy's dead body coiled up next to each other.

"Ty... Ty... it's alright... you can stop pulling... he's dead."

She released the plastic cord only when Barrett grabbed her hand.

Only then did Tyra begin breathing again.

CHAPTER TWENTY

Matt burst through the dairy-farm doors to the outside compound.

The sunlight hit his face.

He squinted, but kept on running.

Most of the living things on the planet could take what came from the sun and change it to something that would help keep them alive.

The vampires were different.

All of them needed a middleman.

And this middleman had broken loose and was now running through the CCC compound.

He sprinted by several goons just standing in place, despite the blaring alarms, apparently with no idea what was going on.

Matt's sprint had nothing to do with a search for a hole in the fence or a place where he could hide until the searchlights were off of him.

"Where did these people think they were escaping to?"

Jay's words reverberated in his head until he had the confidence to stop running.

Planting himself in the middle of the compound, he began kicking his boot heels in the dirt, getting ready to make his stand.

Come and get me, he said to himself. *We're both middlemen, so it's only right you spill some blood along with mine.*

"Hey, mate, what's your name?"

The goon who was serving as the spokesman for the rest of the guards encircling him had an Aussie accent. Hearing his dialect forced Matt to reevaluate his previous assessment about the nationalistic makeup of those working security at the camp. He had assumed that the recruitment of the camp's security staff had been completely filled by locals.

"My name is Matt Haynes and I want to speak to my father and my mother. After I talk to them, I'll let you guys take me."

"What CCC facility are your parents stationed at?" asked the Aussie goon.

"No facility. They're dead. I figured you guys could convey my demands to the undead in charge and then get back to me."

"Come on, Haynes, you know it doesn't work that way."

"Then maybe someone should come over here and explain to me the rules," said Matt. He was moving slowly in a circle, waving his baton.

There was applause, cheers, and shouts of encouragement from the prisoners who had gathered for the showdown.

"That's it, Haynes... show them who's boss..."

"Yeah, man, let 'em all know we're not going to just take this shit..."

"Do this, Matt! We're right behind you!"

As Matt scanned the crowd of prisoners, he didn't see Tyra, Juarez, or Barrett. Nor did he see Murphy. He wanted to believe his diversion had been a success.

Now all there was to do was play it out.

The Aussie raised his baton to his forehead as if he meant for the wood to soak up his sweat. Matt was sure the gesture was a sign that the assault was about to commence.

The first goon advancing toward Matt ran right into a kick that sent him flying backwards, where he wound up landing several feet farther back than where he had first started.

Matt's baton blocked a strike from one of next two guards who rushed him next, then he used the heel of his hand to smash the other goon in his nose. He quickly ducked, just missing a counterpunch coming from the first attacker, and used his baton to swing up and introduce the goon's balls to the wood of his stick.

His peripheral vision caught sight of two more goons rushing toward him. He planted his feet, raised his stick, then tried to swing at the first goon, but Matt's baton was stopped in midair by... Spector.

The Security Supervisor smashed his fist into Matt's face and wrenched the baton from his hand.

Matt staggered, but somehow managed to stay on his feet.

Spector motioned, and all the guards began widening their circle to give their boss more room.

There were shouts all around him, prisoners encouraging him to keep on fighting.

"Give it to him, Haynes!"

"Make the big ape eat a banana!"

But Matt was still groggy from the blow he received from Spector, and all the voices around him sounded muffled, their faces out of focus.

Matt charged Spector, who simply absorbed the blow to his body since there was nothing behind it. He then brought his clasped hands together down on Matt's back, sending him straight to the dirt.

It took almost everything he had left, but Matt struggled from lying flat on the ground... to finally getting up on one knee.

Dietz had just joined the crowd, standing just behind the circle of guards. He watched Matt start to stand, and the doctor said under his breath, "What are you doing? Stay down..."

He rushed forward and threw a wild haymaker. Spector stepped to one side and delivered an elbow into Matt's jaw, dropping the prisoner to the ground.

This time, Matt was out for the count.

Dr. Dietz broke through the circle of goons and tried to approach Matt, but Spector stopped him and motioned for his guards.

"Take him to my office."

***

With Tyra trailing behind, Barrett and Juarez carried Murphy's dead body across the compound as if he was someone they were dragging out to the parking lot from a bar after a long night of heavy drinking.

Because of the chaos Matt had caused, no one stopped them along the way.

No one even looked in their direction as they shuffled Murphy through the barracks' main door.

"Okay, give him to me..."

The three of them, along with Murphy's limp body, were in the close confines of a supply closet that adjoined the shower area.

"Shit, I can't do it by myself," said Juarez.

"Who's the pussy now?" asked Barrett, as he stood on top of a chair holding Murphy's body underneath his armpits.

Every detail of Murphy's death kept replaying in Tyra's head, but each time it played back, there seemed to be a new detail added to the final cut.

"Hey, Ty, I need your help," said Juarez.

Tyra snapped out of her daze, and helped Juarez lift Murphy's dead body up to Barrett. Earlier they had fashioned a noose from the metal electrical cabling dangling from an overhead light fixture. As Barrett guided Murphy's head into the cable noose, he gave his partners careful directions.

"Okay, this is the critical part... we need to be... extremely... careful or I will wind up dying with my arms wrapped around Murphy. Perfect... now just carefully ease him down..."

Murphy's weight activated the initial pin to set up the trap. From there, a series of bedsprings shifted, which then engaged a metal alligator clip, the jaws of the clasp releasing a metal rod covered in rubber bands. The whole contraption was hidden in the ductwork above the ceiling, and was connected to the electrical power feeding the room.

Barrett carefully released the dangling body. He stepped off the chair, still holding his breath, as if he was stepping away from setting up a ten-story house of cards.

"What do you think?" asked Barrett.

Before anyone could answer, he held up his hand.

"Wait, one final touch..."

Barrett reached into the closet and turned the chair on its side.

"Now what do you think?"

"Yeah, that was perfect," answered Juarez. "I totally see Murphy as a chair kicker. He'd change his mind at the last second and say, 'uh… shit… now I can't get my feet back onto…ahhhh…'."

"This totally reminds me of a joke," said Barrett. "How many goons does it take to change a lightbulb?"

"Hopefully, the punch line is at least 'two'," said Tyra.

The sharpness of her answer snapped them both out of their jovial mood.

"I've done this dozens of times," said Barrett. "Of course, I never hotwired the payoff to go beyond a simple electrical shock to whoever tried to remove the dummy."

"So what you're saying is that you're not sure?"

"Well, actually, I am sure. But we'll still need some luck. If just one of the goons tries to take the body down himself, then we'll have two dead bodies, not three."

She nodded and turned to walk away, but Barrett stopped her.

"The trap should work, and get us two more dead bodies on top of Murphy's. Believe me, Ty; I don't want to help that asshole escape unless both you and Juarez are with him."

"For your information, Cliff, that 'asshole' did get the shit kicked out of him… all so we could take out Murphy."

"Good point. I stand corrected," said Barrett. "But how much you want to bet the hotshot had a good time having the shit kicked out of him…?"

CHAPTER TWENTY ONE

<<hamdeanedavanzatiregion>incoming>message<encodedzx>vcnet>>

Greetings Fellow Shadows,

I write today with an enthusiasm that a region representative is rarely able to sincerely feel. It's difficult to limit my emotions to just words, but I will make the effort.

First, join me in celebrating the two latest donation centers which began pumping out their first pints of blood yesterday - CAC29 and CAC18!

Both donation centers, located in the Rakshasis region, were not expected to be online until later this month, but both facilities sent out juice two weeks ahead of schedule.

Help me give a round of applause for the tireless effort of Vivek Asharti, the commander of both CAC29 and CAC18!

Just another reminder that we are all in this together. Those who you trust with your existence could be standing next to you… or a hemisphere away!

Stay Hidden, Stay Silent, Stay Sui Generis!

Very sincerely yours,

Hamil Deane
vc member - davanzati region

***

The capacity for humanity to maintain the semblance of continuity through the direst of circumstances should never be underestimated.

It was one of the points written by a US government official included in a Rangers' handbook that Matt was given prior to being shipped out, with the rest of his unit, to Afghanistan.

The words were in his head as he was being beaten by Spector in the basement area of the CCC officers' security building.

Whenever Spector would crouch before throwing a blow to his gut, Matt made it a point to stare at his oily, acne-filled scalp, on his pumpkin-size head.

After a particularly brutal assault, Spector would stop, hold up his captive's head, and look into his eyes to make sure he was still conscious.

Matt made sure he was staring directly into Spector's eyes as well, fixated on what should have been the white surrounding his pupils, but instead was decidedly yellow.

The world had completely changed, virtually overnight. And yet under the direst of circumstances imaginable, Spector had somehow managed to feed and maintain his addiction to steroids.

His internal laughter at this observation is what Matt used to distract himself from the pain being inflicted upon his body.

"Still hanging in there, Haynes?"

"Yeah, unless you think the band is really done with their set, and then I'd love to use the restroom."

His answer triggered Spector to knee him in the crotch.

The goons who had been holding Matt up let him fall to the ground.

It was awhile before Matt could simply breathe again, but even after he had graduated to that point, his body was still radiating with pain.

"So, you were an Army Ranger...?"

He opened his eyes, but Spector was not standing above him, though Matt was sure it was Spector's voice he had heard based on its high pitch.

The two goons reached down and raised him back to his feet. They turned him around to see their boss sitting behind his office desk staring at a computer screen.

"I thought the Internet went down after the vampires took over?"

"That's right," answered Spector, looking in his direction with a gleam of arrogance. "But you're looking at one of the few on this planet with access to what the vampires put up in its place."

"That's great," said Matt. "Does it have porn?"

The goons holding Matt laughed, but both guards immediately fell silent when Spector turned back to the computer screen without a hint of a smile.

"It says you did two tours. Then you were discharged. You wound up working for some private security firm..."

Matt didn't respond.

"Look, here, sergeant punching bag," said Spector. "We can keep doing this until I either bruise my knuckles or you fucking die. Your choice."

"Maybe if you would let me know what you were after, I could give your knuckles a rest."

"I want details..."

"Details... I don't understand? Are you trying to touch up my obituary?"

Spector leapt out of his chair, marched across the room, then slapped Matt hard across the face twice. The second time, one of the goons lost his grip on him.

When Matt was raised up off the floor of the office, both his mouth and nose had begun bleeding again.

"You're a cancer to my flock." His words were a whisper, but they were spoken with a balled-up fist ready to fly. "What we're doing right now, you and I, is trying to figure out how you got here. Did you come into this camp on your own, or were you sent here by someone on the outside?"

His wanted to laugh in his face, but instead, Matt spit out, "I came with Bunny."

The name got Spector to lower his fist and take a step back.

"We both grew up around here," said Matt. "Just like you. He told me he knew you, had helped you, and that you would take care of us."

Spector looked away.

However, his inner reflection lasted only a few seconds. Then he was right back barking at Matt, just a few inches away from his face.

"You must really miss the Internet, because you are not up-to-date on current events. Everything has changed. Now you either start talking to me about how you were captured, or we're going back in the ring for another thirteen rounds. Now what's it going to be…?"

"What's going on here?"

The tenor of the voice caused Spector to whip around in fear.

Everyone looked around, but no one could see a body behind the voice. It meant there was a vampire standing in the shadows of the office.

"Why isn't this injured prisoner being attended to by one of the physicians?"

Though no one could see its face, Spector knew the voice wasn't Julian's. He responded by directing his answer all around his office.

"Sir, this prisoner ran amok during the blood donation and practically caused a riot."

"Thank you for explaining the circumstances that preceded his incarceration. It still doesn't answer why a donor, clearly capable of manufacturing blood – I'm basing my assessment on looking at his face – isn't being tended to by a physician..."

"Sir, you don't understand; we're in the middle of an interrogation. After I'm finished, I will return the prisoner to the barracks."

The vampire not only stepped out of the shadows, he rushed over to occupy Spector's space. Though neither the head of security nor his goons had ever seen him before, Matt recognized him as his brother.

"Pardon my encroachment," said Ian. "Apparently my razor-sharp hearing is off tonight. I thought I heard you say, 'Sir, you don't understand...'."

"I did not mean any disres..."

Spector's sentence was choked off by Ian's hand, now gripping his throat.

"Ah... so it wasn't my hearing after all. How unfortunate for you, because now we're forced to deal with my hurt feelings, which seem trampled upon, and the only one I saw pacing around this office like a frightened mare was you, Ronald."

"I'm so sorry... sir... but this prisoner ran amok during..."

It was all Spector managed to say before starting to choke...

"Ronny, I can't believe you wasted your final words simply repeating the same details of this man's apprehension. We've already established my hearing is just fine."

Spector tried to respond, but he only gurgled, and choked.

Just as his complexion lost all of its color, Ian released him and Spector doubled over and gasped for air.

"Now, what are you going to do with this prisoner?"

When Spector didn't immediately answer, Ian repeated the question.

"What you going to do, Ronny, with this prisoner?"

Spector was still trying to regain his breath, but it did not matter because Ian grabbed him by the scalp of his hair and struck him hard across the face, causing the head of CCC security to fall backwards. However, he was not allowed to hit the ground, because Ian grabbed him by his jumpsuit, and brought him back up to his face.

"Shall I repeat the question? Or repeat the action meant to increase the speed of your answer?"

"I... return the prisoner to the barracks," Spector managed to answer.

Ian let Spector drop to the ground.

"Brilliant answer. You're starting to prove how smart you are... well, at least 'smart' for someone who has a pulse. Now I strongly encourage you to be the best advocate regarding your intelligence, and follow through on your new strategy..."

Spector barely raised his hand, motioning to his goons holding Matt to take him away. He then turned to spit out the blood that had pooled in his mouth.

When Spector looked back up... Ian had disappeared.

The main door to the prisoners' barracks building flew open and Matt was brought in, then gently set to the ground by the goons.

A couple of prisoners leapt out of their beds to help Matt, but he waved them off.

He stood on his own, gave those who tried to help a nod of appreciation, then stumbled toward the building's restrooms.

Standing at one of the sinks, he splashed his face with water, then looked into the mirror.

Behind him, one of the bathroom-stall doors swung open. It was Doctor Dietz.

"My god, you look awful."

As the doctor approached him, Matt caught sight of the interior of the stall behind him. It was filled with dozens of test tubes, beakers, even a Bunsen burner."What the hell is all that back there?"

As Dietz explained, he began addressing Matt's wounds.

"That's my way of fighting back. Though, I will admit my method lacks the charm of having the bruises and scars that can be used to enliven a good story."

"What do you mean, 'fighting back'?" asked Matt.

"Every creature on this planet has a weakness. We are the apex, and we still have hundreds of weaknesses."

"We use to be the apex," said Matt. "Not anymore."

"Yes, good point."

"Whatever. Are you saying you really have an idea on how to defeat them?"

"No. But I have some theories."

"What do you need to get these theories to the next level?"

Dietz looked at the paper towel he had been using to soak up Matt's blood and laughed.

"Blood for starters. No, not yours. Their blood."

"Matt..."

He turned and saw Tyra standing in the restroom's doorway.

"... you're back. I just heard. Are you alright?"

"Yeah, I'll be fine. We got Murphy, right?"

Tyra nodded. "He's hanging in the supply closet... just like we planned."

"Good."

"Okay… glad you're feeling all right. Why don't we talk before roll call?"

She turned and walked away, but Matt suddenly thought of something and he called out to her.

"Wait… Tyra…"

She stepped back into the doorway.

"Who's the one who ended up taking out Murphy… Juarez or Barrett?"

"Neither… "

Before her reply could sink in, Tyra walked away.

CHAPTER TWENTY TWO

<<hamdeanedavanzatiregion>incoming>message<encodedrexx>vcnet>>

Fellow Shadows,

I'm excited to update the latest on the *STAY ALIVE!* Care Packages which were dropped across the Uppyr and Vjesci regions last week. I can sincerely attest to some guarded optimism regarding the entire *SA!* CP Operation and its goal in recruiting more blood donors. Kudos to VC members Bernhardt, Lochner, and Dedio for their brilliant idea!

Over 20,000 care packages were dropped in the Vjesci region alone, with the following message attached to all the packages:

> *You don't have to be an outlier to stay alive!*
> *Let's WORK TOGETHER!*
> *Join us in our effort to STOP THE BLOODSHED!*
> *Review the included map and use the portable GPS...*
> *And go to the nearest Donation Transport Station near you!*
> *Simply wear one of the red shirts included in this package.*
> *One of our Outreach Teams.will get you to a Donation Center.*
> *And your FIGHT TO SURVIVE WILL FINALLY BE OVER!*
> *You will be taken care of FOR THE REST OF YOUR LIFE!*
> *Your WELL-BEING is our TOP PRIORITY!*
>
> *Included in this package are:*
> *(2) Boxes of Bandages*
> *(1) 8-ounce bottle of Disinfectant*
> *(12) Sterilized Needles*
> *(6) Needles with pre-loaded doses of Morphine*
> *(6) 8-ounce bottles of Sanitized Water*
> *(3) 8-ounce bottles of 97% proof alcohol*
> *(2) 8-ounce bottles of 100% pure Orange Juice*

(1) 16-ounce package of sugar
(2) 16-ounce bags of Beef Jerky.

STAY ALIVE so we can find you and bring you into our care.
Let's all STAY ALIVE on this planet TOGETHER!

The initial data on the *SA!* CP Operation has come in, and as I've already indicated, there is a reason to have guarded optimism. 19% of the *SA!* Care Packages have been moved from their initial drop points. In the last week, 37 living donors visited a Donor Transport Station; and 23 have survived long enough to contribute their first two pints at a Blood Donation Center.

I want to acknowledge those of you who have contacted my staff to strongly suggest that we enact the sonar-homing device located on all the *SA!* Care Packages and begin rounding up the recipients. I will honestly confess to not passing on to the other members of the VC any of your suggestions or objections concerning this operation. The justification for my lack of letting your views be known is because I firmly believe that this operation has just begun, and we must wait and see the results before concluding that it has not been a success. Furthermore, by activating the homing devices to zero in on all of those who have the care package would destroy donor trust and preclude any similar operation in the future.

At this time I simply ask for the patience of everyone who doubts the wisdom of this operation.

To the rest of you; thank you for your positive messages and encouragement!

Stay Hidden, Stay Silent, Stay Sui Generis!

Very sincerely yours,

Hamil Deane
vc member - davanzati region

***

IAN HAYNES' JOURNAL

Do you remember Mr. McCutchen? We both had him for science in Junior High School. I don't think he would have changed his lesson plan in the two years that separated us, so I'm betting you heard about his discussion of vampire bats and how their daily behavior has taught us about the concept of altruism.

Each night, vampire bats leave the cave and look to feed. In the morning some return without any success. Vampire Bats will die if they do not get a meal two nights in a row. That is why the bats who were successful in feeding that night, will then regurgitate some of the acquired blood and share with those bats that need to still feed. Underlying this whole nightly dynamic was that those bats who were successful one evening might not be successful the next night, or next week, so they share, and expect the same kind of treatment in the future. This is what Mr. McCutchen called an example of "Altruistic behavior in the animal kingdom." He considered it a sign that humans, like most animals, like vampire bats, were altruistic in nature.

However, years after we both graduated, there were new findings that challenged the foundation of the study that formed the basis of Mr. McCutchen's lesson plan — scientists have documented that the sharing of blood from one bat to another has been shown to only occur when the bats were related, as in the same family: mother to child; child to parent... brother to brother.

This is known as kin selection, not altruism.

I wonder if Mr. McCutchen revised his lesson plan.

I have written many of these entries with the idea that perhaps you will one day be reading this. But I have to say, after last night, I should lower my expectations that you will ever get the opportunity to read these words. Matt, you should know that what I did for you was beyond the call. And yet, how was I rewarded?

I left Spector within seconds of your exit. I wanted to see if your walk to the barracks building would bring just a moment of recognition of what I did for you. I won't claim to have saved your life: the head of CCU47 security knows better than to kill a healthy donor.

But still, imagine my disappointment when all I witnessed was a conversation about the Lakers and the Nets between you and the guards. Never mind that everyone that once played professional basketball is dead. I speak of just the very idea that you would engage in a meaningless conversation with two nobodies while my latest effort to save your life goes completely without acknowledgement.

Tonight I put a little "blood" in your mouth so you could live and you would see the love that I still have for you. My effort was rewarded with complete ambivalence.

My entry today is a recounting of what preceded the following vow to myself — I will make no more efforts to help you avoid the fate of most of humanity. I had set aside the experience of our initial meeting, believing it would be too early to judge any of your words as definitive. But now you've had time to reconcile recent revelations and your actions are a testimonial to your feelings regarding our relationship — I died ten years ago... and as far as you're concerned... I'm still dead.

***

Ian told the Outreach Supervisor working for him that he would depart from the rest of the patrol and search the Morristown Canals for possible donors.

It was a lie so Ian could get away and be by himself.

After everything that had happened recently, all Ian could think about was to hide.

His first choice was a place he remembered playing with his brother Matt when they were younger. Standing in one of the canal tunnels, he hoped to take in the same breath of air they both breathed so many years ago.

When he emerged hours later, a fog had settled over the turbine incline plane near the Stewartsville canal station. It took him a few moments to realize that Winston was standing nearby. Ian was "startled" in a way that only a vampire understands.

Rarely does a human fail to alert another vampire of his presence, long before they share the same space. And all vampires, at least those who have been properly taken under wing, know the essential courtesy of sending a signal of approach before sharing the same space.

"Sir, you surprised me?"

"I am so sorry, Ian," said Winston. He then shut his eyes and would not open them until he finished with his apologies. "Please, forgive me for not making my presence known earlier."

Ian replayed back in his head his actions for the last several hours.

Satisfied there was nothing his mentor could have seen that would bring him shame, he replied, "Sir, you did not offend me in the least. Besides, whatever you choose to do, I am here to listen to your reasons…"

It was only then Winston opened his eyes.

"Well, I must confess, that I've been here for quite awhile observing you."

"You've never questioned my habits, nor my spirit to serve your desire," said Ian, as he stepped over some exposed Roebling cable and onto the sleeper stones that ran for miles along the route of the canal. "You must have had cause to observe my behavior," continued Ian, now standing just a few feet away from his mentor. "As I said, I am here to listen to your reasons…"

"Will you walk with me? Along the way, I will try to explain."

They moved through the woods, proceeding in such a way that their presence could not be observed, except for a few species with a beating heart.

Their mode of travel covered a great distance. Ian never suspected that Winston was guiding them toward a specific destination as they spoke.

His mentor steered their conversation toward experiences they had shared together prior to the takeover. Ian trusted that Winston had a purpose to the memories he had sorted through, selected and was now recounting. He was certain that everything had been carefully deliberated over.

Winston's extractions invited Ian to voice his recollections as well. However, the more they recounted their shared past, the more Ian became confused. There seemed to be a bigger point underlining the direction and focus of Winston's words, but Ian could not deduce enough of his mentor's aim to imagine the target.

"I recently hinted at the circumstances concerning the turning of your brother, Julian, but I did not offer any details…"

"Since time is never an issue, I assure you, sir, that I was not impatient. You were distracted, if I recall," said Ian.

Winston chose that moment to stop their travel, and all around them the world came back into focus.

"I am not distracted now," said Winston. "Indeed I am focused in a way that I have not been in a very long time."

"Sir, are you… all right?"

Winston grabbed Ian and yanked him closer, "Tell me the truth. Do I not look… alive."

"Yes…sir, you do indeed look alive."

They both smiled, and the grip on Ian's arm turned gentle.

"I have never shared our experiences with anyone else. Nor do I choose to share the experiences I have had with Julian. Only he can choose to share those experiences with you. But I want to tell you something because it is time you knew…"

He paused, as if he heard something in the distance, but whatever drew Winston's attention did not change his demeanor as he continued to speak to Ian.

"There is another that shares my blood. Our blood. I turned her… and Julian at the same time. But it was only because of her that I embarked on the reckless act of turning Julian."

Winston tightened his grip on his arm and pulled Ian to him. He kissed the side of Ian's neck, his lips resting on the original scar, before he whispered, "there are two final fates waiting for all of us. Only those with an imagination are able to choose…"

He released his arm, and Ian staggered backwards. Perhaps if he reclaimed some space between them he could think clearly about the words that had passed between them.

"Sir, I apologize," he finally said after a long silence. "But what you have said… your words… they are overwhelming me…"

Winston nodded his head. "It is to be expected. The words I have spoken to you will resonate only when you understand them first. However, Ian, that will take more than just… *time*."

There was a voice from afar. And it was then Ian understood why Winston had paused earlier. He had always said, "those that walk with my blood, I can hear walking a mile away."

"Winston… Ian… why are you standing there? I thought I was very clear where we were to meet…"

The voice engulfed Ian in a way that Julian probably wished he could wield over everyone, especially his kind. Despite the impending presence of his blood brother, he whispered to Winston, "Sir, what is happening?"

But Winston answered his question with a question: "Our kind. How are we defined?"

His question was the beginning of a mantra spoken traditionally as a dialogue between two vampires.

"Our kind are not defined by death," answered Ian.

Winston recited the next line, "But our existence is dependent on the living."

"What must we do to justify taking the blood of the living so we may exist?" asked Ian.

"We must give back to the living at least what we take in return…," said Winston, but Ian noticed his mentor's eyes had lost focus midway through his answer and he was staring off into space.

Ian was troubled, but he continued, reciting the last line of the dialogue.

"… or we are a kind that should have embraced extinction when it was offered."

"What are you two doing!" shouted Julian, as he walked up to them. "The sun will be rising soon and I don't feel like racing back to the compound. C'mon, I called you out here for a reason. I've got something to show you both…"

Winston did not hesitate. He began following Julian as he walked toward a mountain that had a halo of orange smoke drifting just above it.

When he realized Ian had not kept up with them, Winston turned and motioned to him. "Come along, my son; the three of us are so seldom all together."

CHAPTER TWENTY THREE

The prisoners stood in line for the morning head count.

Each roll call had two CCC guards assigned the duty of coming up with a matching head count.

"I got 165. What about you?"

"I think I got 165...."

"Jesus, Fonty, did you or did you not get 165?"

"You know I'm not even supposed to be out here. Polasky has a hangover and asked me to cover his shift."

"Yeah, well, Polasky with a hangover can still count better than you."

Brandon, the compound shift supervisor, stepped up to the two guards, Helske and Fontaine, to get their head count numbers.

"Guys, give me the count."

"165," answered Helske.

"Yeah, I also got 165," affirmed Fontaine.

"165? Are you guys sure?"

Both guards nodded.

"Fuck me. Spector is going to freak," Brandon mumbled to himself.

He then stepped away from his underlings to address the prisoners.

"Okay, I need your attention. Which one of you juice boxes is missing?"

When there wasn't an immediate reply from the assembly, Brandon shouted out, "Whoever helps me, I will make sure to return the gesture…"

"Yo' momma."

The words were loud enough for the three goons to hear, but too low for any of them to finger one particular prisoner.

"Who the hell said that?" shouted Brandon as he scrambled up and down the lines.

"Sir… I think it's Murphy missing," said Barrett.

Brandon immediately ran up to him. "And why do you think that?"

"Because he is usually standing with us, but now he's not. Sir."

The prisoners who heard Barrett's answer smiled.

"Sir, I heard Murphy speaking about how he missed his momma."

The shift supervisor brushed by Barrett to get in Juarez's face, because the way Juarez enunciated the word "momma" left little doubt who had shouted out the insult earlier.

"Why don't you say, 'Yo' momma,' again, Juarez," said Brandon.

"No… I couldn't possibly top the way you just said it, sir," answered Juarez.

Everyone around the guard and prisoner snickered.

"Okay, Juarez, what exactly did Murphy have to say?" asked Brandon.

"Hard to make out exactly, sir. He was doing most of his crying in the shower and it was hard to hear, you know, with the water going, and the soap in your ear."

Fontaine turned to Helske and Fontaine.

"Find him. Now. And bring his sorry ass back for a whipping."

The two guards had been searching in the barracks building for over twenty minutes, when Helske let out a yell.

Fontaine followed the voice down the hallway near the showers area. He discovered his shift partner standing just outside the supply closet with Murphy's body hanging from the ceiling.

"Is he dead?"

"No, Fonty, he's just sleeping in," answered Helske.

"Hey, it's a fair question," protested Helske. "Who the fuck knows anymore?"

Brandon was pacing back and forth behind the assembly. He glanced at his watch, and almost swallowed his tongue when he saw the time. He couldn't put it off any longer, he needed to wake Spector and give him the bad news.

Then there was the sound of tapping on glass, and Brandon rushed over anxiously to see what Helske was motioning for him to see.

"Fuck me. Had to happen on my shift!" Brandon mumbled to himself. "Get him down from there," Brandon shouted through the window at Helske.

Fontaine was the one up on the chair, trying to lift the body through the loop. Helske was standing a few feet away hoping his partner wouldn't need his help.

"Sorry, this guy is kind of a load. I'm going to need a little intervention here."

Helske sighed, wrapped his arms around the body's legs and lifted him up.

The alligator clip, attached to the wires, closed around the metal rod, setting off a series of sparks, which then surged into a full-blown fireworks show in the closet.

The two goons violently shook as thousands of volts of electricity shot through their bodies.

Spector and Brandon entered the building and immediately saw smoke drifting down the shower hallway. They rushed to the supply closet and discovered that both of the early shift guards had joined the suicide victim, not only in death, but also in appearance, as all three corpses looked like meat left overnight on a flaming BBQ.

***

Helske's body was set down on the ground next to Fontaine.

Both bodies were just a few feet away; neither had yet been bagged because Spector wanted his entire security team to see the full glory of what had happened to them.

Matt couldn't believe it, but Spector was totally playing into his plan. He was almost afraid that some of the other prisoners, already suspicious, would now believe he had struck a deal with the head of CCC security.

"Look at them. This could be any of you," yelled Spector at his guards. "I will tell you one thing, it won't be me."

He grabbed the hair of one of his goons with such force that the guard lost his footing. Spector dragged him the rest of the way and stuck his nose into Fontaine's burnt corpse as if he were training a misbehaving dog that had just shit on the living-room carpet.

"Smell that? That's what stupidity smells like!"

The prisoners were intentionally milling about close to where the bodies had been laid, near the cadaver van.

Matt had rehearsed with the others two different distraction scenarios he had been taught by veteran Army Rangers on his first tour. But Spector was making all of those preparations redundant.

The goon who'd had his nose rubbed into the crispy corpse of his recently departed colleague was finally released by Spector, and he crawled back to the rest of the assembled guards.

But Spector wasn't finished with his demonstration. With a menacing sneer, he withdrew a hunting knife from his belt and marched toward his team.

The first to break from the security assembly was the one Spector made a point to pursue. After chasing the guard down, Spector subdued him, then raked his blade across the skin of the goon's arm.

While this was happening, both Helske and Fontaine were put in body bags by a pair of CCC guards. Dietz zipped the three body bags, then motioned for the guards to load them onto the cadaver van. After all three bags were loaded in the back, the guards moved to join the security assembly, but Spector's angry voice stopped them in their tracks... just a few feet from the cadaver van

Matt, Tyra, and Juarez had no choice but to continue to wait to board the vehicle.

A heavy hand landed on Matt's shoulder, causing him to wince. He was still healing from the beating he took from Spector.

"Oh, did that hurt. I'm really sorry about that," said Barrett. "I guess I keep on forgetting what you've sacrificed for all of us." He then bent down so he could whisper in Matt's ear. "Want to know the truth...? I still think you're going to jackrabbit on us once you get beyond the main fence."

He tilted his head away from Barrett's warm breath on his skin. "I got your point the first time. You were wrong then. And you're wrong now," said Matt.

"I hope so," said Barrett, using his big paw to squeeze Matt's shoulder. "It'll save me from spending the rest of my life hunting you down..."

The second guard to break from the assembly was chased down next and dragged by the collar of his black jumpsuit across the compound. Spector then planted the goon right next to the guard he had sliced with his knife.

"There you go. Now start sucking..."

"Sir?!"

"You heard me, start sucking his blood!"

When they hesitated, Spector grabbed for his knife, but that's all he needed to do, because the second goon suddenly leaped forward. He fastened his lips on the bleeding arm of his fellow guard and started sucking like his life depended on it.

The way Spector hovered over the pair watching, perhaps it did.

The whole spectacle had the two guards, standing near the cadaver van, terrified they would trigger Spector's wrath. They sprinted over to join the rest of the assembled guards, even though the van's doors were still wide open.

It was the opening the prisoners needed, and they formed a wall of seemingly interested observers while Matt, Tyra, and Juarez hopped into the van.

Matt specifically went for Murphy's body bag. The last thing he wanted was for Tyra to be riding next to him.

Juarez unzipped Helske's body bag, and the sight of the goon's twisted, grisly body caused him to flinch.

"Oh, my god, that smells horrible. What the hell did this guy eat before he died?! I'm not doing this…"

Tyra had already unzipped her body bag when she realized Juarez was serious.

"We don't have time to argue!"

"No one said anything about spooning with a dead guy," whispered Juarez.

"You either get in the fucking bag now," said Tyra, "or, I promise you, you'll be getting a bag all to yourself when I get back."

Juarez looked over at Matt.

"I'll trade you for Murphy."

Matt's response was to zip up Murphy's body bag around him.

Dr. Dietz shut the van doors, and the engine of the cadaver van started up.

Juarez did a quick air cross, then took a deep breath before climbing inside.

Spector was wrapping up his demonstration to his team of guards.

"If the prisoners start killing themselves, it will only be a matter of time before our overlords start looking for replacements for their blood supply.…"

The goon had stopped sucking on the other guard's arm wound. Spector noticed, rushed up, and delivered a hard kick in the ass.

"You keep on sucking his blood until I tell you to stop…"

After the guard began sucking again, Spector resumed his speech.

"I'm not confident any of you truly understand our potential future. That's why I took the time to show you."

Spector moved to the guard sucking on the arm, and raised his head by grabbing onto the guard's mullet. There was blood smeared all over his mouth like a toddler who had been eating his first strawberry-jam breakfast.

"This won't be me. If you don't want it to be you, then you'll get your shit together, now!"

"Sir, did you call me over?" asked Doctor Dietz.

"Yes, one of my guards has sustained an injury that I need you to attend to…"

Dietz looked back just as the cadaver van started to pull out of the compound.

"Of course sir, I'll address this at once…"

"No, take your time," said Spector. "The way these fuckheads are doing their jobs, they're all going to be dead anyway."

Spector then stormed off.

CHAPTER TWENTY FOUR

<<hamdeanedavanzatiregion>incoming>message<encodedzzlxx>vcnet>>

Greetings Fellow Shadows,

I wish I was writing to you with more upbeat news, but I am seated on the VC only at the grace of those of you who believe in my will, and continue to support me through these troubling times.

An unfortunate turn of events has forced me to announce that negotiations between the so-called "red wing" and "black wing" factions have broken off.

At this moment, I would characterize the possibility that the two wings will resume talks and reach a compromise as more than doubtful.

Indeed, I will characterize the situation by repeating a word that someone on one of the wing factions used during a heated argument in the middle of negotiations…

The word is "floating."

I must admit I felt very offended, at hearing the word spoken aloud, not only because of the context, but also because the speaker who uttered the word did so as if he was perfectly entitled to not only use the word to support his argument, but that he should feel comfortable in allowing the word to leave his lips in such a casual manner.

Simply put, there are those amongst our kind who believe that because we all share a similar existence, we all have had a similar experience. And that is simply not true.

At the expense of offending those who need not defend their knowledge of what the word actually means, I will lay down a few details of background for those who cannot claim such experience.

There was a time when travel between the different regions meant weeks of isolation on board a ship, which often forced the hand of a shadow who wanted to simply survive.

Killing one crew member of the ship could be hidden. The draining of two crew members might have gone unnoticed if it was cleverly handled, but the loss of blood from three members of a ship's crew would, without exception (I'm drawing on the personal experience of four transatlantic, oceanic journeys), trigger a full-scale witch hunt from rudder to anchor.

Anyone who even looked like they had red in their cheeks would be keelhauled or receive twenty lashes before being set adrift.

"Floating" is the word those of us with personal experience came to use to signify the beastly survival tactics one must employ when forced to utilize the blood from the other "passengers" of the ship, who would not be missed.

None of those experiences are looked back with any pride. But it is we "floaters," living off of the blood of rats, who have enabled many of you to be reading this at all. Forgive me for coming off as "old school," but unless you've actually had rat hair stuck between your teeth, I do not believe you are qualified to use the word in any context, no matter how much you claim your policies will alleviate suffering amongst our kind.

Stay Hidden, Stay Silent, Stay Sui Generis!

Very sincerely yours,

Hamil Deane
vc member - davanzati region

***

"We both wondered where you've been, Julian?"

"Wondered why? All you needed to do was look out the window. Are you saying neither one of you caught my performance?"

"Actually I watched every second," answered Winston. "I grant you your 'performance' had a certain style, but I must temper my compliment with a concern that perhaps you've missed recent VC directives, especially those emphasizing the severe worldwide shortage of healthy blood donors."

"So you don't see the strategy in killing a few so that the others would be intimidated, thus guaranteeing long-term cooperation?"

"Julian, I'm afraid intimidation only guarantees, not cooperation, but the necessity of its chronic use as a strategy."

"Very disappointing to hear," said Julian. "Especially since I shot the entire assembly on video. I planned on playing back the deaths of the escapees on the monitors in the barracks' building every night before the prisoners all went to sleep. So you would not agree that it would be effective in maintaining discipline?"

"Perhaps there would be a short-term cause and effect," answered Winston. "But I don't believe such a tactic would engender a healthy stress level amongst our blood supply."

Ian was shocked by Julian's reaction to Winston's verbal chastisement. His blood brother seemed almost excited by Winston's negative response.

"I predicted almost everything you would say," said Julian. He pulled out a note from his coat and held it up for Winston and Ian to see.

True to his word, almost everything Winston had said was written verbatim on the paper.

"I was only off by one word, 'perhaps,' said Julian. "I would never have dreamt you would use the word 'perhaps' in criticizing my behavior. You know something, I believe, old man, that after 221 years, I'm beginning to wear you down."

Winston laughed and then answered without hesitation or reservation.

"Yes, Jules... perhaps you are."

The three then brushed aside tree branches leaning across the path before emerging on the other side of the hilltop. The sight of what lay in a gully below caused Ian to stop walking.

It was a huge, deep pit dug into the earth. There were huge flames jetting at least a hundred feet into the sky, creating a billowing cloud of orange and black smoke that rested like a crown above the pit.

"What the hell is this?" asked Ian.

"Pretty extraordinary isn't it?" shouted Julian as he rushed up to the pit like an excited young child approaching a new playground. "One of the demolition teams at this site exposed some gas pipes. That's when one of the factions in the VC decided to point their initial plans for the area in a different direction."

Winston moved to the pit and looked down. The glow of the pit fire lit up and highlighted the distinct details of Winston's face, in a way that Ian had never seen before. Despite his earlier words, it was a moment where Ian admitted to himself, *Now, my mentor, truly does look alive.*

"Sir, you've read the statistics generated by the VC," said Julian. "Do you disagree with their findings?"

"No, Jules, one is a fool…"

"… to argue with VC statistics," said Julian completing Winston's sentence. "Old man, I will always respect how you were consistent in what you taught me and how you acted. I will also appreciate all the words you have passed on from those who existed before us. What did you used to say, ah, yes: 'those who fail to rise above the mistakes of the past, are…"

"… simply animals behaving as predators or prey," said Winston, completing Julian's sentence. "C.Q. Yarbaro is who you are quoting. I actually know her."

The words "predators or prey," provoked Ian to awaken from the trance he had been in since he emerged from the woods. His eyes caught sight of something he noticed for the first time – the wooden stake, normally attached by a chain, was no longer around Julian's neck.

"Where's your needle?" asked Ian, while at the same time springing forward to step between Julian and Winston.

Julian kept his eyes fixed on Winston as he responded.

"Right here…"

The wood was from Easter Island. Or so Julian claimed. Taken from the last tree originally grown on the island.

Before Ian could stop him, another hand reached out. He looked over and discovered Winston holding onto him.

"It's all right. We need to let your brother finish his presentation…"

Winston then turned his gaze toward Julian.

"Is this what you need to do?"

"No, sir," said Julian, before he lunged forward, brushing past Ian as he shoved the wooden stake all the way through Winston's heart.

"This is what I *want* to do…"

He nodded several times, as if his neck was now a spring attached to his head. Then Winston turned to look at Ian, but there was nothing left to his face but skin over bones.

Ian felt the hand gripping him suddenly release a moment before Winston leaped off the ground and took flight.

He flew about a dozen yards over the pit before his wings suddenly vanished.

Then Winston began to fall.

A chorus of cries erupted from below as Ian scrambled to the edge of the pit.

For the first time he saw what lay beneath the flames that stretched toward the sky.

There were the bodies of his kind, writhing in pain and screaming in agony. Thousands were stacked on top of each other, all finally dying the death that some had put off for years, others for centuries, and those special ones who were now embracing the day they often referred to as the "crow's crooked beak."

Through his tear-filled eyes, Ian saw there were those among the dead and dying who reached out their skeletal arms to welcome Winston as he landed amongst them.

"Careful, brother, you might fall," Julian said, hoisting Ian by his neck and finally releasing him about a dozen yards away from the edge of the pit.

Ian swept his hand across his face, wiping away the tears before he looked up to lock eyes with Julian. He could not believe the first thing that was staring at him was the wooden stake with Winston's blood dripping from it.

Julian saw Ian's reaction, and immediately dropped the stake into the dirt.

"It's not what it looks like. He stepped away, and I held on for some reason. Please, Ian, do not believe for a moment that I wanted the instrument of his death as some sort of souvenir…"

"What have you done…?" screamed Ian.

"What needed to be done, brother," Julian calmly responded. "You're too young to understand. That's why I could not share with you what needed to be done."

Ian stumbled to his feet, "Yes, you're right; I don't understand."

The words were spoken with such passion that Ian stumbled… into Julian's arms.

"But he understood! Didn't you see his face? Our father understood!"

Ian pushed away from Julian and fell to the ground.

"Love!" he screamed into the night. "That's what I saw. Love for the two he had turned…"

"No, what you saw was acceptance."

Julian's voice was flat and unemotional.

"But the sun will be rising soon, so we haven't the time to debate the issue."

He tried to walk off, but Ian shouted after him, "Why did you do this?"

Julian looked up to the night sky and screamed. "He promised me heaven… and he did not deliver." Suddenly, Julian was standing at the edge of the pit. "What you witnessed tonight was my decision not to follow Winston into hell."

Ian closed his eyes.

When he opened them again, Julian was standing above him.

"I am promising you heaven. Or you could follow the source of our immortality as he discovers the contours of hell. What shall it be?"

Ian bowed his head.

"Good for you, brother; the acceptance of final death is something very few vampires rarely see in another, and yet you are wise enough to have seen it in Winston's face."

Ian looked up and saw that Julian had moved away again, speaking as if he was addressing some crowd that had gathered to hear his words.

"All I ask as we move forward is to understand the burden I shouldered in making this difficult decision. The VC purge has begun. Yes, decisions had to be made. And those in charge decided to go with 'new blood'."

He turned and held his hand out toward Ian.

"Come and let us bond in a way that we've never been able to bond before, building upon the death of a man who led to our rebirth, so that we may have a new relationship."

Rising, Ian tried to make it seem as if he intended to grab Julian's extended hand.

"My heart feels like it is beating with possibilities," said Ian, as he pitched forward to grab the bloody stake.

Out of nowhere, one of Julian's support team snatched the carved wood from the grass.

"Is this what you used on him?"

Ian looked around him and saw that the entire group had come to check things out.

"Drop it, Vadim – now, or I will use it on you," shouted Julian.

Vadim carefully set the stake back into the dirt and backed off.

Julian was now standing just a few feet away from Ian, and yards away from the edge of the pit.

"Please, brother, do not let their presence sway your emotions. I ask that your loyalty be earned, because we share the same blood, and because it is the right thing to do, not because another choice has been closed off to you."

Ian did not hesitate. Julian would only fixate on the hesitation, and who knows what his mind would do with such a thought rolling around in his brain every waking minute of every waking day for the next hundred years.

He embraced his brother.

The energy emanating from Julian's every pore astounded Ian.

When they parted, Ian turned to Julian's followers and made sure his face did not have a hint of menace. He now believed that their sudden appearance prevented what would have been a futile attempt to avenge his mentor.

CHAPTER TWENTY FIVE

Matt kept time with his watch as the truck left the concentration camp. He knew of the perfect spot where the three could bail from the cadaver van.

He unzipped his body bag and looked around.

The cargo hold was closed off from the front cab, so they did not have to worry about the driver seeing them. Matt shivered, realizing for the first time that the back of the van was refrigerated.

"Okay, guys, let's go, this is our exit…"

Immediately both zippers started moving, as both Tyra and Juarez squirmed out of their bags.

"That experience might have put me off on ever breathing again," whispered Juarez.

Matt had told himself to expect a lot of blather from Juarez, and not to let it get to him unless his bullshit threatened to get them caught.

He moved to the van's back doors to have a look, and as he suspected, the moment they opened the doors, there was no doubt it would trigger a light on the dashboard of the truck.

"How are we doing?" whispered Tyra.

"Right on time," answered Matt as he looked at his watch. "Are all three bags sealed?"

"Yeah, exactly like they were before we got in," answered Tyra.

"Wait, I didn't read my goon a bedtime story; should I…?"

"Shut the fuck up," Matt harshly whispered to Juarez. "No more of your bullshit until we get back to the camp. Are we clear?"

He nodded.

"Okay, it's just like we talked about; as soon as I open this door, we'll need to jump out and then move quickly to the side of the road. No excuses. There's a good chance the driver will stop. Are we clear?"

Both Tyra and Juarez nodded.

"Tyra, you're first, then you Juarez… I'll be right behind you both."

He did a silent countdown… then threw open the doors.

Tyra did not hesitate; she leaped out of the van the moment she saw daylight.

Waiting for Tyra, Juarez had some time to gauge the speed of the van, but when Matt waved to him, he rushed forward and jumped out.

Matt followed two seconds later.

He hit the pavement and pain shot through his legs. He tried to stand, but gravity pushed him forward and he went with it. Matt tumbled several times, then tried to stand again; this time his lower limbs responded and he began moving toward the side of the road. As he rushed toward the embankment, he looked behind him and saw no sign of Tyra and Juarez.

The cadaver van suddenly halted.

He leaped and landed into some tall weeds.

There was the noise of footsteps, then a door closing. Seconds later, the van started back up and the noise of the engine grew more and more distant.

Silence.

"Matt…?"

Tyra helped him up out of the bushes. Juarez was standing next to her.

"I can't believe we made it," said Juarez.

"Well, hold off on texting your friends," said Tyra. "We still have a lot to do before we make it back to the compound in time for roll call… right, Matt?"

She didn't realize that Matt was already moving toward the woods.

"How are we doing?" Tyra asked when she finally caught up.

"None of us should relax," answered Matt. He was jogging and looking all around him. "I've seen plenty of vampire patrols working during the day. They won't be at their strongest, but it doesn't mean they won't be here."

"So you know where we are?" asked Tyra, almost out of breath after just running less than three hundred yards.

"I know exactly where we are," answered Matt.

He then switched gears and moved off at the base of a valley and into the woods that lay adjacent to the road.

Tyra stopped to wait for Juarez to catch up with her. They both then took off in pursuit of Matt.

"Help me out here," said Juarez, catching his breath in between every half dozen words. "Do we need to tip the guide who is leading us on a prison break?"

***

"Hey, Matt, can we slow down the pace a bit?"

Matt turned and, rather than feeling perturbed, he looked embarrassed. He stopped and waited until Tyra joined him.

She turned to see that Juarez was still about twenty paces behind her, but close enough that they both started jogging again.

"Sorry about that. I was caught up in my mind gaming out all of our moves."

"Ah, a clue to how your mind works," said Tyra, still catching her breath. "So when you say 'gaming out all of our moves,' are you talking from start to finish?"

"I wish," Matt answered, but that was all he said.

After they continued to run in silence, mostly because Tyra still needed to regain her breath, she finally followed up with another question. "I guess what I'm asking is, do you try to work out everything to the final outcome?"

"I used to try and do that," Matt said. "But there are too many variables."

"So you stop at a certain point?"

"No, I just mentally follow the path until it divides into several options."

"Then what do you do?" she asked.

"I make sure there are no other options besides the ones I'm considering."

"And then what?"

He stopped running.

"Did you ask your father and brother all these questions?"

"Yeah, as a matter of fact, I did."

After her answer, the two continued running along the path through the woods in silence.

Tyra figured it was either because he didn't have an answer to her original question, or because she shut him down with the way she answered his question.

Finally, he spoke again.

"I've been meaning to tell you something, but I haven't had the right opportunity," said Matt. "What happened with Murphy… is not what I intended."

"Are you saying you didn't game it out?"

He looked at her to see if she was joking with him or taunting him.

"I guess what I'm saying is that I didn't think long and hard enough to come up with all the options."

"So you're saying you would have done things differently?"

Matt went silent again. For a while all there was between them was their breathing.

"I've done things," he finally said. "Obviously things I've been able to live with. And this could have been one of those things. That's why I should have been the one… not you."

She was looking at him as he spoke, wondering how much he himself believed was true.

"Well, it's done," Tyra said. "So there's no use talking about it anymore."

He suddenly stopped running. They stood there catching their breath.

Matt looked at her, but she knew it was not with eyes that were checking her out in a good way. He was evaluating her to see if she had recovered from what happened in the dairy building. His eyes ended up locked on her eyes only so he could see if she was up for the task at hand.

"Hey, Mom, Dad, the movie is over. Are we there yet?"

Tyra wanted to scream when she heard Juarez's voice, but before she could respond, Matt turned and said, "Yeah, actually, we are…"

***

Matt had made sure they approached the farm from the back. They looked all around the compound, but there was no sign of anyone around.

He made his way to the front entrance of the barn and gently opened the doors a crack. Matt looked around and, strangely, it was like everything that he once remembered in the barn had been kept perfectly as it once was.

Juarez pushed open the door behind him, and the noise triggered two birds to emerge from their nest in the rafters. They both made a quick beeline for a shattered window near the barn's loft.

Tyra peeked in and said, "How are we doing, Matt?"

"We'll find out in a second. My mother and father had some ATVs they used to move around the farm."

Matt grabbed a large, beige, canvas tarp and yanked it toward him like he was unveiling a new statue to patrons at a museum.

Underneath the tarp were four ATVs, two of which had trailers behind them.

It took a few tries, but Matt was able to get the first one fired up.

Juarez got the second ATV started with just one kick.

Matt reached out a hand for Tyra to join him on his ATV.

"Don't I get one of my own?" she asked.

He turned to look at the older ATVs.

"Those are the ones my brother and I used to ride on when we were kids. I can't trust they'll make the trip to Halcyon Ridge and back."

She took his hand, swung her leg over the seat, and sat down behind Matt. Tyra then wrapped her arms around his waist as he released the clutch and eased the vehicle of out of the barn.

As they moved through the back road to Halcyon Ridge, Matt eventually realized, after looking at their faces, that there was a huge difference between what he was feeling, and what Tyra and Juarez were going through.

Sure they were only going twenty-three miles an hour, the top speed his parents' ATVs could go while pulling trailers. But for two people who had been locked down in a concentration camp for more than six months, used to getting chased for two pints of blood twice a week, the breeze on their faces and the open road ahead of them still added up to something that was close enough to qualify for a feeling of... freedom.

CHAPTER TWENTY SIX

They parked both ATVs in the main square of Halcyon Ridge.

"I bet this place was dead even before the takeover," said Juarez"

"Yeah, pretty much."

"Are you all right?" Tyra asked.

"Concerned," said Matt as he looked at his watch. "About the time."

"I hear you," she said. "So why don't we prioritize? Weapons first; food and drinks second; then more weapons third."

"I love the philosophy," said Matt. "But we'll need to squeeze in one more thing on the agenda."

"Lead the way," said Tyra.

He pointed across the street.

As they moved closer to the Bulls-Eye Gun Gallery, Tara noticed the confident swagger in Matt quickly dissipated. When Matt reached for the handle of the front door, the wind actually brought it toward him.

Entering the place, the three stepped on a floor covered with shards of broken glass as they looked all around them and saw the firearms shop had been completely cleaned out. Every glass case had been broken into and was empty. All the gun racks lining the walls were polished-wood veneer, looking barren and pointless without the rifles meant to complete them.

"Ooops…"

Tyra punched Juarez in the shoulder.

"Why do you have to be such an asshole!"

"How is 'Ooops' being an asshole?" protested Juarez. "I wanted to say, 'Maybe I should check in the back room just in case someone left behind some slingshots or boomerangs,' but I pulled back because I know we're working as a team here."

She was almost afraid to look over and see how Matt was reacting, but he suddenly turned to them.

"I need you to both go further up, about fifty yards, and on this side of the street you'll see a knitting shop on the second floor above the town's historic museum. When you enter the shop, go directly to the back room, but when you go in there, there will be two doors: one is the bathroom, but the other door leads to a small room where you'll see a mess of shelves loaded with jars of jam and preserves. Grab as many as you can and load them into one of the ATV trailers."

"I don't understand; are we going to a bake sale after this?" asked Juarez.

Matt looked away and took a deep breath. It was either that or he might have taken a swing at Juarez.

"You know there's a general store just down the block," said Tyra.

"Beanes' general store is going to look just like this. I'm sending you to a place that looters would not think to look. My ex-wife knew Katy Melton, and I've seen all the preserves she keeps in her far back room, because it's completely out of the sunlight." Matt looked at his watch. "You both just need to do what I say. We're running out of time."

Then Matt rushed past them. He was about to leave before Juarez shouted after him.

"So let's say we get Aunt Bee's preserves, what then? Is the plan to throw the empty jars at the vampires when they come after us...?"

"No," answered Matt as he turned around in the doorway of the shop. "I have a backup plan, but it means making another stop when we head back to my parents' farm. That's why we need to move. I'll meet you both back across the street in thirty minutes."

He then dashed off.

Juarez took a few steps toward the door and mockingly yelled, "Nice to have met you. Call me, maybe." He turned to Tyra. "We're fucked!"

"No, we're not," she quickly replied.

"Barrett was right... he's totally going to jackrabbit. I can't believe you don't see that."

She stepped past him, on her way to exiting the shop. "Let's go, we're going to do exactly what he told us to do..."

Juarez shook his head, but followed. However, he needed to have the last word. "So what you're saying is that you completely missed the cotton tail that was clearly pinned to his ass when he left..."

***

She looked at her watch. It had been thirty-five minutes since Matt rushed off.

Juarez had his finger in one of the jars – peach cobbler – and was tasting it.

"Stay here…"

He quickly sealed the jar and stood up.

"Where are you going?"

Tyra had been anxiously wondering where Matt was when she saw movement on the second floor of a building directly behind the parking lot where they had their ATVs parked.

"He's in there…"

She started to walk away toward the red-brick building, but he stopped her.

"How do you know it's not a vampire…?"

"Because it's not. Now I need you to stay here. Go back over and crack open a jar of lemon-curd preserves, but be here when we get back. I mean it, Juarez."

She stepped through the broken front glass of the main entrance to the building. Piled just a few feet away were several crates of bottled water and a stack of medical kits. It immediately made her feel better as she sprinted through the main lobby, up the stairs, and onto the second floor.

The official government offices of Halcyon Ridge had originally encompassed a pair of two-story buildings. But five years back, when the town hit hard economic times, the local principality was forced to lease out one of the buildings to companies in the private sector. It meant moving all the records for nearly three centuries into a single room on the second floor.

This is where Tyra found Matt, moving frantically from one filing drawer to another. She was about to go in and tell him that whatever he had been looking for he should give up on, but then he stopped slamming drawers and muttering under his breath. Whatever he was looking for, he found. Matt unfolded some papers and set them down on a table in the middle of the room and fell silent.

"What are you doing?"

"Hey… were the preserves there?"

She entered the room and moved toward the table. "Yeah, just like you said. We loaded a hundred jars of jams into one of the ATV trailers."

"Great. And I found some water and medical kits…"

"I saw them when I came into the building."

"People forget that every government office has to be prepared for an emergency."

Tyra was now close enough to see that it was blueprints spread out on the table.

"This is where we're being held prisoner…"

He nodded, clearly relieved that he had finally found what he was looking for.

"Yeah, the old Army training facility in Morristown, New Jersey."

"Nice call. This will really help us in our escape," said Tyra.

Matt suddenly blanched when he saw the time on his watch.

"Shit! We got to go…!"

***

"There's something that I haven't been able to forget. Something you said…"

"Yeah, let's hear it…"

The three of them were driving back to his parents' farm from Halcyon Ridge.

Once again, Tyra was riding behind Matt on one of the ATVs.

"It was when you told Tulliver and Chast that I grew up around here…"

She waited, but since she couldn't see his face, Tyra had no idea Matt was finished speaking. So she said, "I don't understand what you're trying to say, Matt."

"When I first arrived at the concentration camp, and we talked, I never said I grew up around here…?"

She had her arms around his waist. Tyra tried not to let loose or squeeze any harder before she answered.

"Are you sure you didn't say anything?"

"Positive. So how did you know?"

Tyra thought about what to do, what to say, until she couldn't wait any longer. She tightened her arms around him.

"It was that night in the Green Zone, in the basement of that hotel bar." Matt shouted into the wind. "I told you where I grew up… right?"

She laid her head into his back and then nodded…

"That's what I thought. Okay, you need to hang on because this is our turnoff…"

Matt raised his hand for Juarez to see. He then veered off the paved back road they had been travelling on to and from Halcyon Ridge.

Their ATVs rumbled onto a dirt road that cut through an area with huge lots broken up with dense woods. Most of the lots had one-story houses, each one at least forty or fifty years old, but there were a few with just a trailer parked in the middle of overgrown grass.

He motioned to Juarez, and they parked the two ATVs in front of one of the last houses adjacent to the base of a mountain.

Matt got off the ATV, and immediately turned to help Tyra off.

She was holding his hand when he said, "Let's go inside."

The three stepped onto a wooden porch. As Matt checked to see if the door was unlocked, she noticed that there was nothing on the porch except a bucket filled with several inches of cigarette butts.

The living room had been ransacked, just like Beth's house, but Matt didn't take long to digest the mess before he was moving toward the back of the house.

With Ty and Juarez closely behind, he entered a room that looked relatively undisturbed compared to the rest of the house, perhaps because there wasn't much to the room – no closet, and only two pieces of furniture: a desk and a chair.

There was also a rug in the corner of the room. A Muslim prayer rug.

Matt went straight for the rug and pushed it aside, revealing a trapdoor in the floor. He saw Ty and Juarez looking at the prayer rug with curiosity, and said, "It's nothing, just Rocco's sense of humor." Matt then grabbed the handle and lifted the access door to the cellar.

"Forget about that. It was just Rocco's sense of humor."

He led the way down a flight of stairs that unfolded with the opening of the basement door. Lights automatically switched on when Matt moved past a sensor built into the wall.

As soon as he confirmed that what they had come for was actually still there, Matt turned to look at Ty. He knew that she was walking into what Jay used to call: a "classic bad news, good news scenario – Your beautiful daughter comes home at 3:00 a.m., but she's holding a Bible in her hand. How do you react?"

The entire 60 X 80 basement was filled to the gills with weapons of individual destruction. Firearms lined the walls, some stretching through the ages, but mostly just the last ten years – automatic weapons bought, traded for, stolen, taken off a dead body, all now hanging on hooks like trophies from a big-game hunter.

And not just guns.

There was an entire wall taken up with axes, knives, swords: so many sharp instruments, that after viewing half the collection, a Benihana chef would have to sit down before he fainted from too much excitement.

There was even a corner of the room completely devoted to explosives. Grenades of every kind, from World War One to the Korean War. And plastic explosives were on display. Some in the original packaging, several on a table with the wires dangling from the clay.

Matt was surprised that neither Ty nor Juarez said anything as they walked around, like they were being courteous to the other visitors enjoying the exhibit at the museum.

Finally, Ty spoke. "You knew this guy…?"

She asked her question while staring at photos that adorned the wall next to the weapons.

DRAWING BLOOD
211

Before he could answer, she pulled a photo off of the wall, one depicting Rocco hoisting a huge stein of beer, while the pub table in the foreground had two pistol machine guns next to a pack of cigarettes and a mobile phone.

She handed the picture to him and Matt saw that Rocco wasn't the only one in the photo. His arms were wrapped around Matt and Jay.

***

It had started to get drafty in his parents' barn by the time they got back with their haul of weapons and supplies. Matt tried shutting both of the doors, but the broken windows above were still allowing the wind to kick through the barn.

"We're going to need something to hold this tarp down if we're going to hide some of the weapons in here," said Tyra.

She was obviously asking for Matt to come up with a solution, but she wasn't looking at him.

"What about a staple gun?"

He waited for Tyra to look up, but realized that was not going to happen. She had not looked at him straight in the eyes since they left Rocco's house. Tyra even chose to ride with Juarez on their way back to his parent's farm.

"Yeah, that should work," said Juarez. He didn't bother to make eye contact with him either.

They had food... water... an armory of weapons... all because of him.

Now Tyra and Juarez couldn't even bother to make eye contact with him.

He moved to his father's work bench and opened up several drawers. Finally the contents of one of the drawers got his attention. There was a bottle of booze, several packs of cigarettes, a framed photograph… and a shotgun.

Matt picked up the photograph. It was a picture of him, Ian, and his father. Everyone was mugging for the camera with big smiles.

He stared at the photograph.

"Find that stapler?" shouted Juarez from across the barn.

Matt walked over and tossed the stapler to Juarez. He then turned to Tyra and tossed her something as well, which landed at her feet.

A pack of cigarettes.

She looked at the cigarettes and smiled.

"Now we're square," said Matt.

There was a cold, distant tone to his voice that got Tyra to look up. She saw that he was holding a shotgun. And the expression on his face didn't look right.

Tyra stood up. "Matt…"

"Stop right there," he said to her.

Before anyone could say another word, there was the noise of a loud thud on the roof.

CHAPTER TWENTY SEVEN

During the initial days of the takeover, Matt and Jay had received some intelligence from the people back in Virginia. It was what they had been able to put together regarding their own employees' experience against the vampires, and what they were able to gather from other sources.

There were five combat capabilities the "FSF" intel reports rated as 90 percent or higher that "the adversary" possessed. One of the five was that a vampire was capable of convincing an enemy target that a noise was coming from a different source or direction.

Somehow Matt completely forgot about the intel report as he waited breathlessly for the vampire to make his entrance from his parents' barn roof.

With his shotgun pointing up, Matt was taken completely by surprise when the side of the barn exploded like a bomb had gone off. A shard of the barn siding caught Matt in the head, sending him to the ground, dazed.

From her belt, Tyra snatched an Al Mar knife she had planned to take back to the concentration camp, and raced toward Matt. When she saw a shadow moving toward her, she slashed at it, sending her off balance and stumbling forward.

After regaining her footing, Tyra saw blood dripping from the blade of her knife.

The creature was no longer a shadow, but now was standing about a dozen feet away, bleeding from the chest. The blood from the wound was soaking up the black T-shirt the vampire was wearing.

This was not anything like Tyra's previous experience in fighting a vampire, which occurred on the night she had been captured. The wound she inflicted on a vampire from one of the blood patrols healed so quickly there was almost no blood loss.

A shotgun blast sent the wounded vampire into the air. It landed on the ground near the opening of the barn.

"Are you all right?" asked Matt.

Tyra nodded, keeping her eyes focused on the still body of the creature that now lay two dozen feet away.

"How about you, Juarez?"

"I'll feel better when we stake him."

"The both of you stay right where you are..."

Matt started to confidently walk toward the creature. Blood was pooling up all around what looked like a heap of human body parts that had been stacked on top of each other.

But as Matt drew in closer, he saw bubbles in the pool of blood... and that convinced him that this encounter was far from over.

Suddenly, the pile of body parts all seemed to reorganize in a flash, and there was a vampire leaping toward him.

Matt reacted by calmly pulling the trigger.

The shotgun blast propelled the creature backwards with enough force that the impact threw open the barn doors.

He stepped out of the barn, reloading his shotgun as he kept one eye on the vampire lying in the ground just a short distance ahead. After he fed the last bullet into the chamber, the vampire rose slowly in front of him.

Matt took aim, but rather than shooting at something he expected would be moving toward him, the vampire was fleeing across the farm compound.

He narrowed his eyes to re-aim, but then a twenty-foot stream of fire streaked across his eye line. It looked like an orange lightning strike coming from out of the woods, which immediately set ablaze the vampire that had been trying to escape.

The creature stumbled for a few feet, then fell into the dirt. It rolled around, emitting a squeal of pain before falling silent and still.

Two figures, standing at the edge of the woods surrounding the farm compound, began advancing toward the fallen creature. Both were cradling flamethrowers.

Matt made his move toward the vampire as well. As he drew in closer, he held the shotgun over the creature, but after seeing its condition, he realized there was not going to be another resurrection. He stepped away and lowered his gun.

"Good choice. Dead is dead this time."

He was fairly sure that he recognized the voice, and turned.

One of the figures behind the flamethrower removed the headgear and goggles, and then pulled off a cap that had been keeping her hair in a bun.

It was a woman dressed in camouflage clothes, with smeared, black shoe polish all over her face.

"Beth. I thought that was you…"

He was referring to the voice, not anything else. His ex-wife had changed quite a bit since he last saw her. Her eyes were so intense; the pupils looked capable of becoming bowling balls and rolling him over like he was the last pin standing.

She also had long, taut arms, with bulging veins; both limbs seemed as if they weren't just holding the flamethrower, but that they were appendages originally built into the weapon.

"Yeah, I recognized you too the minute I saw the shotgun," said Beth. "Your father's old rifle, right?"

He looked at the gun, and almost couldn't believe that he was now holding it with Beth just a few feet away.

"How about that?" said Matt. "The same gun I had when I tried to kill myself."

Beth froze when she heard the words.

"Come on, that's what you were thinking, right?"

A long time ago, Beth figured out that Matt had a way of framing his questions so that any of her answers would be channeled in just one direction: the quickest way to triggering his temper.

"That's him…"

The other person holding the flamethrower approached. He took off his goggles and the rest of his headgear.

"… Yeah, I'm pretty sure this is the guy I saw that night at your house."

Matt looked the guy over and said, "If you're still not sure, why don't you get out your flashlight and fucking shine it in my eyes."

His tone and the words were like a magnet, pulling Ryan to take up the space right next to Matt.

"Tell you what. Forget the flashlight; why don't you just raise your voice loud enough to attract a vampire patrol."

Beth stepped between them.

"Matt Haynes this is Ryan Sellers. Yes, Ryan, this is my ex. Matt, what are you doing here?"

"I saw the restraining order against me had lapsed. I figured getting it extended was not an option under present conditions. So I decided to make my way out here. How are you doing?"

"Well, she just got done saving your life," answered Ryan, moving past Beth to get closer to Matt.

He kept his eyes focused on his ex-wife. "I'm sorry, I might have missed something. Is Ryan your lawyer?"

"I'm not her lawyer, but I'm also not fucking with you."

He then nudged Matt with the nozzle of his flamethrower, which was still fired up and ready to go. "You need to dial back the attitude, Haynes. As I said, she fucking saved your life. Maybe you crawled back under the rock you originally came from during the takeover and missed the information about how vampires absorb bullets like a sponge. There's only a few ways to kill them, and shooting them with a shotgun is not one of them…"

Matt listened to every word Ryan had to say before breaking out in a grin.

"Sorry. My mistake. Beth has saved my life so many times, I guess I'm guilty of taking it for granted," said Matt.

He then stepped around Ryan's flamethrower, and began walking toward the barn. Matt was relieved when he saw Tyra and Juarez moving toward him.

"You didn't answer my question," said Beth. "What are you doing here?"

After he got over the shock that Beth was pursuing him, he got angry.

"This is my parents' farm; why do I need to explain anything to you?"

"That's bullshit, Matt, and we both know it. You were at my house," said Beth. "I'm asking for you to explain why you were there!"

He stopped walking and turned to face her.

"I was looking for you. I wanted to make sure you were safe."

"Safe? Don't make me laugh. I can take care of myself. And second of all, taking care of myself got way easier the day I stopped taking care of you."

"Are you all right?"

Beth turned to look over at Tyra.

"Yeah, I'm fine," said Matt.

All the tattoos on Tyra's body immediately grabbed Beth's attention. She then noticed that Tyra's skin was also lined with vampire bite marks.

Tyra grabbed his arm and this time Matt looked over at her.

"We need to get going."

Matt stared at Tyra.

"Matt, we need to get going."

He nodded, and without another look at his ex-wife, Matt turned and started walking toward the barn.

Beth tried to follow, but Tyra stepped in front of her.

"I don't know who you people are, but we don't have time for this."

"Nice," said Ryan, walking up behind Beth. "We just saved your life, and that's all you have to say?"

"No, I'd like to add three words of gratitude," said Juarez. "Flame on, Dude!"

Beth moved closer to Tyra, and lowered her voice. "I know that guy, and I'm warning you, he's someone you all need to stay clear of…"

Tyra pulled a cigarette from the pack Matt had tossed to her in the barn. She used the flame on Beth's weapon to light it up.

"Matt and I go way back. We worked together in the Green Zone." She took a long drag on the cigarette. "Right now we're right in the middle of trying to set free about two hundred people from a vampire concentration camp."

Tyra took another puff and then blew some smoke into Beth's face,

"So, thanks for saving our lives. But if you don't mind, you need to get out of the way because you're fucking up our plan to sneak back into the camp…"

She then threw down the cigarette, stamped it out in the dirt, then hit Juarez in the back and they both left to join Matt.

He walked slowly into his parents' barn and embraced the darkness that was beginning to descend on the hilltop where he grew up.

Matt had traveled across the world to see if the love of his life was alive. On many nights during the trip, he actually spoke aloud the words he would say to Beth if she was somehow still living. And every night during his trip back to Morristown, New Jersey, he would rehearse those words while staring at her picture.

"The world's come to an end and I came back to see if you were still here, hoping if I found you… that somehow you and I… we could start all over again…"

TO BE CONTINUED…

BOOK #2 THE RELICT SERIES:
"Shadows in the Light"

MORE INFO AVAILABLE
ON
"DRAWING BLOOD"
&
THE RELICT WORLD

RELICTBOOKSERIES.COM

YOU'LL FIND THE LATEST NEWS
ON THE MOST RECENT BOOK
PLUS A TON OF BACKGROUND
ON THE RELICT WORLD

WORDS, PHRASES, AND WISDOM
THE SHADOWS HAVE SHARED WITH EACH OTHER
FOR THOUSANDS OF YEARS.

BIOS OF THE MAIN CHARACTERS IN "DRAWING
BLOOD" & THE RELICT WORLD

FSF INTEL REPORTS SENT TO MATT HAYNES

BACKGROUND INFO ON "THE TAKEOVER."

AND SPECIAL SURPRISES READERS WON'T GET
ANYWHERE ELSE!

FIND OUT MORE ABOUT THE RELICT WORLD
RELICTBOOKSERIES.COM

APPENDIX

THE
CHIMES
BEFORE
MIDNIGHT

I

Believe your existence matters in this world.
But never live like you are the center of the universe.

II

Our life on this planet is relatively short.
Some we love will have an even shorter life.

III

Beware of predators amongst us who kill or maim.
Sometimes with no discernible reason.
Someone we trust, even love may be one of the predators.

IV

The greatest challenge we face as individuals…
(and as a Species)
…is to continue to EVOLVE.

V

There will come a time when the opportunity to…
Solve a Problem, will no longer be an option.

VI

When you are younger pursue a dream.
If you don't end up achieving it…
You will still discover yourself in the process.
And you will put aside any future thoughts…
… of what might have been.

VII

Live your life with honesty and integrity.
At all times.

VIII

Discover who you truly are…
… beyond the expectations of family, friends, loved ones…
… and those you have just met.
It will mean working to overcome your fears.
The fears that come from within…
… and those created by family, friends, loved ones…
… and those you have just met.

IX

We need others to thrive and reach success.
Your future depends on those across the street…
… as well as the person you've never met…
… who lives across the world.

X

You need to love and be loved.
You will not reach your fullest potential without both.
Everything else is forgotten over time.
Those you loved, and those who loved you…
… will be your legacy on this planet.

XI

There will be those who are dependent on us to survive.
We must not neglect their needs.
A climb to the mountain top is worth celebrating.
Unless the goal could have been achieved...
... while carrying another on your back.

XII

As you age, never live without another worthy goal.
But don't allow the love of life...
... to be corrupted by the fear of death.

IT IS MIDNIGHT

There might be someone beside you.
Or no one to bear witness.
Regardless of the circumstances...
ALL of us face death... ALONE.

You are not the center of the universe.
After taking your final breath...
Every living creature on this planet...
... will take another.

CHIMESMIDNIGHT.COM

ACKNOWLEDGEMENTS

Franklin Guerrero

Thanks to Larry & Hemmi, the retired guards from the defunct Lorton Maximum Security Prison. They gave me unique insight into prison life and even braved the asbestos warnings to take me to the bowels of the "off-limits" areas. This knowledge and imagery was invaluable to me as we created our vampire prison camp. Also, thanks to my mom and dad for always encouraging my artistic endeavors. And to Debbie for being patient with me through the years as we put this together.

Richard Finney

Much appreciation for everyone at Lono Publishing and their support. I would like to especially send kisses to Brad and Jan who never stop following "the light." Special thanks to the editor of this book, Katy Sozaeva, who worked hard on meeting our timeline. Of course to Danuta for her ongoing support. Much appreciation to Luke Vitale who would not let this story die. Lastly, a special thanks to all those readers out there who have been so supportive with my past work. Your online reviews, feedback, and passing the good word on to other readers has been so wonderful. Specifically I want to mention, Shay, Stephen, Kitty, Terry, Duchovney, Mitzi, and Rebecca. You all rock! All of you have made storytelling worth the effort.

ABOUT THE AUTHORS

Richard Finney is a Southern California based writer, film producer, and screenwriter. He is the author of the novels *Demon Days* and *DEMON DAYS – Angel of Light* (both co-written with D.L. Snell). *The Cake is a Lie* is a collection of his short stories. He is also the author of a graphic novel, *The Wind Raider* (written with Dean Loftis).

Visit his website -- richardfinney.blogspot.com

Franklin Guerrero is an award winning filmmaker with a deep appreciation for the world of horror and SF. The films he has written and directed include *The 8th Plague* and the cult classic, *Carver*. He lives in Southern California. *Drawing Blood* is his first novel.

For more info on Mr. Guerrero - relictbookseries.com